NELL SCHOFIELD

Nell Schofield presents films on the subscription television channel *Showtime* and writes about classic movies for Melbourne's *Sunday Herald Sun*. A graduate of NIDA, she has worked as an actor as well as reporting on the arts for organisations such as ABC TV, ABC Radio National and CNN International. She is the female voice on ABC TV's *Media Watch* and is contemplating writing a film script tentatively titled 'The Revenge of Freda the Moll'.

For Simon Drake—another young film star
who lived to tell the tale

AUSTRALIAN SCREEN CLASSICS

puberty blues

NELL SCHOFIELD

First published by Currency Press Pty Ltd and ScreenSound Australia in 2004.

Currency Press Pty Ltd
PO Box 2287, Strawberry Hills
NSW 2012 Australia
enquiries@currency.com.au
www.currency.com.au

ScreenSound Australia
National Screen and Sound Archive
GPO Box 2002, Canberra
ACT 2601 Australia
enquiries@screensound.gov.au
www.screensound.gov.au

Australian Screen Classics series: ISSN 1447-557X

National Library of Australia—Cataloguing-in-Publication Data:

Schofield, Nell
Puberty Blues
Bibliography
ISBN 0 86819 749 1.
1. Puberty blues (Motion picture). I. ScreenSound Australia. II. Title.
(Series: Australian screen classics).
791.4372

Cover design by Kate Florance, Currency Press
Front cover shows Nell Schofield as Debbie and Jad Capelja as Sue. Back cover shows Julie Medana as Kim, Sandy Paul as Tracey, Joanne Olsen as Vicki, Leander Brett as Cheryl, Nell Schofield as Debbie and Jad Capelja as Sue. Both photographs courtesy of Umbrella Entertainment. www.umbrellaent.com.au
Typeset by Currency Press in Iowan Old Style roman 9.5 pt.
Printed by Hyde Park Press, Adelaide
The DVD of *Puberty Blues* was produced by Umbrella Entertainment.

AUSTRALIAN SCREEN CLASSICS

JANE MILLS
Series Editor

Our national cinema plays a vital role in our cultural heritage and in showing us what it is to be Australian. But the picture can be blurred by unruly forces including competing artistic aims, inconstant personal tastes, political vagaries, constantly changing priorities in screen education and training, and technological innovations and market forces.

When these forces remain unconnected, the result can be an artistically impoverished cinema and audiences who are disinclined to seek out and derive pleasure from a diverse range of films.

Screen culture, of which this series is a part, is the glue needed to stick these forces together. It's the plankton in the food chain that feeds the imagination of our filmmakers and their audiences. It's what makes sense of the opinions, memories, responses, knowledge and exchange of ideas about film.

Above all, screen culture is informed by a *love* of cinema. And it has to be carefully nurtured if we are to understand

and appreciate the aesthetic, moral, intellectual and sentient value of our national cinema.

Australian Screen Classics will match some of our best-loved films with some of our most distinguished writers and thinkers, drawn from the worlds of culture, criticism and politics. All we ask of our writers is that they feel passionate about the films they choose. Through these thoughtful, elegantly-written books, we hope that screen culture will work its sticky magic.

Jane Mills is an Honorary Associate of the Art History and Theory Department at the University of Sydney, Senior Research Associate at the Australian Film, Television & Radio School, a Board Member of the Sydney Film Festival and is the recipient of a scholarship at the Centre for Cultural Research, University of Western Australia.

CONTENTS

ACKNOWLEDGMENTS

Love and thanks to Jane Mills who breathed deeply and pushed until this bun came out of the oven without too much toxic green icing. Thanks also to Margaret Kelly, Kathy Lette, Gabrielle Carey, Bruce Beresford, Don McAlpine, Geoffrey Rhoe, Daniel Mudie Cunningham, Unjoo Moon, surfie chicks Meagan Edwards and Victoria Manaro, Rosemary Curtis, Emma Blomfield, Darren Mansfield, Elizabeth McMahon, Lesley Speed, Germaine Greer, ScreenSound Australia, Greg Gurney ('scragdaddy'), Jad Capelja, Craig Hassall and Boomi.

Nell Schofield, 2004

Illustration acknowledgements

Thank you to the following for permission to reproduce the following images:

Umbrella Entertainment: cover, and pages 6, 9, 18, 19, 33, 43, 47, 51, 53, 60, 69 and 82

Limelight productions (sourced from ScreenSound Australia): pages 52, 67, 75 and 84

Nell Schofield: pages 2, 32, 54, and 55.

1

SURFIE SCRAG

It's something I'll never live down. Practically every week over the past two decades or so somebody comes up to me and mentions it: 'You were in *Puberty Blues*! Oh my God! That film changed my life!' Not only that. These freaks know all the best lines, like 'fish-face moll', 'rootable' and 'you're dropped'. And it's not just women of my generation who flip out over the film. I recently interviewed an all-male rock band with serious street cred and the guitarist could hardly answer my questions because he was so busy raving about how cool he thought the film was. The other day, a fifteen-year-old girl went all weak at the knees when she met me and her mother had to explain that the kids regularly hold *Puberty Blues* parties. As do older folk.

It seems that dear old *Pubes* has even become something of a fashion statement. Not long ago I was walking past one of those trendy street wear stores, and did a double take when I saw a silhouette of myself and co-star Jad Capelja printed on a sexy little T-shirt with a handbag and wallet to go with it. I went in immediately to buy the matching beach towel as a souvenir. Twenty years on and a photo of two girls in the sand dunes, one

Retro Surfie Scrag: the look du jour

carrying a surfboard, is the height of teen chic. Retro Surfie Scrag, it would appear, is the look du jour.

So why does this particular Australian film continue to strike such a resonant chord with so many diverse people? Is it the fact that it presents a youth sub-culture that they can all relate to? Is it the language, raw as a radish and unashamedly Australian that people find so endearing? Perhaps it's just a time capsule of Australian life in the late 1970s that people both embrace and are repelled by at the same time. Or maybe it's the triumph of the under-dog that ultimately wins them over, that classic story arc which sees the protagonists reject peer group pressure in favour of individualism? Here are a couple of factoids to mull over: *Puberty Blues* is listed number 41 of the top Australian films and number 17 (along with *Gallipoli* and *The Sum of Us*) on the list of Top Rating Australian Feature Films screened on television.[1] But it seems the film has moved beyond these statistics into a realm that borders on cult.

Obviously there are creative technical factors that contribute to the movies' durability too, not the least of which being the crafty direction by Bruce Beresford and lensing by his acclaimed colleague, Don McAlpine. These two men had worked together on *The Adventures of Barry McKenzie* and the follow up, *Barry McKenzie Holds His Own,* both celebrations of bad blokey behaviour and peculiar Aussie vernacular. The pair also collaborated on *Don's Party, Breaker Morant* and *The Club,* more iconic films revelling in Australian manhood. For almost a decade before embarking on this teenage surfie saga, Beresford and McAlpine had been developing a visual language that often worked in counterpoint to the earthiness of the scripts, adding touches of poetry where on the page there was only gritty realism. For these two 'New Wave' filmmakers, *Puberty Blues* was a major departure from their usual fare. They were plunging head on into the chick flick genre and with all that oestrogen pumping about they had to keep a steady grip on the viewfinder.

Puberty Blues is a story about two Sydney teen babes muscling their way into a top surfie gang then busting out of it again with renewed confidence and independence. In essence, it is feminist tale; the girls initially try to fit into the narrow, stereotypical roles assigned to them but eventually realise that the whole scene 'sucks'. In defiance, they do the unthinkable and take to the waves, invading a strictly male dominated space. The honesty of the material and its insight into Australia's urban surfing world is unique.

Its originality lies in the racy book of the same title by Kathy Lette and Gabrielle Carey who, aged 18, wrote a no holds barred account of their early teenage years and let it loose on the public much to the delight of their fellow teens and the scandalised horror of their parents. Kathy's mother, Val, was particularly appalled. She was the Principal at a school in the Sutherland Shire where the tale is set, and took it as a personal affront, an assault on her reputation. As Kathy later explained:

> ... the publication of *Pubes* must have been an excruciating embarrassment for her, especially where the pinstriped-underpanted parents were concerned. She brazened it out, but things were a little bit frosty, all right, arctic, at the time.[2]

These two surfie chicks told it like it was for them trying to break into the Greenhills Gang at Sydney's Cronulla Beach; the gross initiation ceremonies, being paired with boys they'd never even met and joylessly losing their virginity in the back of panel vans at drive-ins. They disguised themselves in the characters of Debbie and Sue but few were fooled and, as Gabrielle Carey subsequently revealed, the book was 'totally autobiographical'.[3]

I first read it soon after it was published in 1979 when a friend thrust it at me in the playground one day. I had already heard about the two authors. They were notorious, a wild double act lunging at life like there was no tomorrow, biting off more than they could chew and chewing like buggery. They called themselves 'The Salami Sisters', the idea being that they were doing something 'spicy and meaty'. Not only had they written this outrageous book but they were also writing a column in a Sunday tabloid, the *Sun*

Herald, called 'A Slice of Life' and running around the country as Spike Milligan's self-proclaimed groupies.

Flicking through the book, I could hardly believe my eyes. Not only was it rude, lewd and utterly spot on as far as the current teen lingo went but here was the story of my life... well, not exactly but pretty damn close. It was hilarious and horrendous all at the same time—full of things I knew only too well because I too had been drawn to the sexy, salty, sandy, sun-tanned world of the beach, only in my case it wasn't Cronulla but Bondi. And just like the narrator in the book, Debbie Vickers, I had an inseparable bosom buddy. Debbie had Sue, I had Emma, a friend without whom I would never have dared to do half the things I did in those heady formative years.

We had gravitated towards one another at primary school when we were both about ten and were later accepted into Sydney Girls' High School. She was everything I was not: blonde, tanned, pretty and popular with all the boys. She had an older brother and could relate to the opposite sex whereas, coming from an all-girl family, I found them totally alien. We first caught the 380 bus down to that iconic crescent beach in 1976. The smell of tropical suntan oil and the spray off the waves was intoxicating. Girls lay sprawled topless on their towels, their erect nipples courting the gaze of passers-by, their bronzed legs bent just so ... to reveal their inner thigh. And then there were the boys: the pecs, the tight bums, the stringy blond hair, the sight of them all glistening wet in the sunlight as they stripped out of their wetsuits to reveal their scungies. The term 'budgie smuggler' has since come into popular use to describe this vision but back then words simply weren't enough. The sight was captivating and my eyes gobbled it up in a manner not dissimilar to artist Tracey Moffatt in her ironic perv

The Greenhills Gang boys

fest video *Heaven* which could well have been based on this excerpt from Lette and Carey's book:

> The art of changing in and out of boardshorts at the beach was always done behind a towel ... The ultimate disgrace for a surfie was to be seen in his scungies. They were too much like underpants. The boys didn't want us checking out the size of their dicks.[4]

On the very first page of *Puberty Blues,* we are introduced to the hierarchy of the beach. Debbie and Sue start out as 'dickheads' occupying the lowly area of South Cronulla Beach along with the migrant family groups and kids from the western suburbs known as 'Bankies' – short for Bankstown – where many of them lived.

Em and I weren't exactly dickheads, or 'westies' as we called them, but we weren't in the top gang either when we first made our moves on Bondi. There was, however, a similar delineation of zones. The coolest of the cool hung out on the hill above South Bondi with the best view of the waves. There was another gang, the Rock Crew, who oiled their bulging biceps around an exposed rock just down from the southern-most ramp off the promenade. These guys surfed a bit but mostly they were interested in modelling menswear and plucking the spunkiest chicky babes off the sand. Way down at the northern end of the beach was Dagsville—no one ever surfed there unless the swell was really pumping. To begin with, we were on the periphery of the gangs at the south end. Our little group hung around the third ramp behaving badly. I've got a photo of one of the boys chucking a browneye for the camera in full daylight: so very mature. All summer long we had fun, tanning and swimming and watching the boys surf. Just like the girls in the book.

When winter arrived it was as if nature suddenly threw a big soggy dampener on the whole beach party. Em and I, however, were not about to be shut out of the fun that easily. We were thirteen and raring to go so we got ourselves jobs working as waitresses at the Sunshine Inn at North Bondi serving up Hunza Pie and spiralina shakes and saved up to buy ourselves surfboards. Ten dollars bought me a beaten up six foot Graham King, Em got herself an eight inch longer McCoy, and in May 1977 we took the plunge, crossing over that gender divide between the sand and the surf. There was perhaps only a couple of other female surfers braving the waves back in those days so we definitely stood out. At first we could hardly balance on the boards and were ridiculed mercilessly by the guys. But soon we were hooked, if not obsessed, and would go out in the most gnarly conditions like dedicated kamikazes. The boys finally caught on that we were 'dead set' and stopped bagging us. We'd get up at 3 am in the pitch dark before the buses were running and walk the five or so kilometres to Bondi to catch 'the early'. Nothing was so liberating as being out there in the dark water overcoming our fear of sharks and watching the sky slowly change from black to blue to pink to yellow to red. We were morphing into soul surfers and before too long we'd managed to slide up the hill to hang with the other cool grommets.

The next year, after just ten months of dedicated wave action, we were featured in the surfing magazine, *Sea Notes*.[5] There were two big photos with a caption that proved prophetic, at least for me: 'We're going to be actresses'. There was also a quote from Em, which read 'On Thursdays we can surf through first period. It's only scripture'. The interview, we announced, was setting us back about two hours of beauty treatment time but surfing was something that needed promoting: 'It's so gas. It's just really free', I said. The only trouble was the outfit: 'It's a bit of a hassle in bikinis because they slip everywhere and you've tits flying everywhere... you get stared at too'. Asked if there was anyone that we wanted to surf like, I named one of the most radical surfers of the day: 'Gerry Lopez. No women idols because you never see any. I've never seen any film clips of women surfers... these chauvinistic films I dunno'. We had seen films like *Hot Lips and Inner Tubes* and *Tubular Swells* but no women featured in them. We were carving out our own patch of urban ocean and before long I was Treasurer for the New South Wales Women's Surfing Association. I even entered the Pepsi Golden Breed Pro Junior surfing tournament and was interviewed on 2JJ – as ABC's youth

Debbie's famous pigtails

radio station was then called. But surfing was not without its hazards and I was the victim of a fin chop which required eleven stitches, five of which I still have in a scrapbook.

That year, aged fourteen, I fell in love with a macrobiotic poet surfer called Daz. It was deep. We ordered brand new matching surfboards and hitch-hiked up the New South Wales coast to camp and surf at all the legendary spots: Crescent Head, Angourie, Byron Bay. Our soundtrack that summer was from Albie Falzon's seminal surfing film *Morning of the Earth*. Songs like 'Simple Ben' and 'Open Up Your Heart' went round and round the cassette player 'til they almost erased themselves. Every other soul surfer worth their board wax was tuning in to the same magical music, making it the first locally-made film soundtrack to go triple gold.[6] Daz, three years older than I, was reading Patrick White's *The Tree of Man* for his school exams while I was reading *Spiritual Midwifery* in preparation for my role as Earth Mother. My father took decisive action and on my fifteenth birthday moved me to an all-girl private school where the uniforms were a suitably boy-repellent shade of olive green.

I was like a freak of nature, dumped in the middle of this posh scenario with my three massive diamante studs in one ear lobe, not to mention the weirdo hairdos I'd been fostering at Sydney High (hairdos that were eventually to find their way onto Debbie Vickers' head in *Puberty Blues*). For a while I continued to go to the beach, surfing before and after school but increasingly schoolwork took precedence. Worse still, I began to like it. But when this slim, racy book was furtively shoved into my hands in fifth form (Year 11 as it's now known), I heard the primal call of the wild once more.

Debbie and Sue had it much rougher at Cronulla than Emma and I did at Bondi. They moved from Brandivino to marijuana when they were just fourteen whereas I was still pinching bottles of Riesling from my father's cellar to guzzle outside the Bondi Regis Hotel. While we were losing our virginity to the surfies of our dreams in tents pitched up the coast at Iluka, the girls in the book were hanging out at Panel Van Point, 'the deflowering capital of southern Sydney'. One thing we did have in common, though, was that we were all several years under the age of consent and seriously sexually active. Like it or lump it, hormones run rampant during that touchy-feely period known as puberty.

I gobbled up the book in less than an hour then later re-read it in bed to make sure I'd really seen what I thought I'd seen—words like 'pash', 'root', 'tit-off' there in black and white for all to see. Worse still, 'fucking', 'gang-bang' and 'she sucks a mean cock'. These Cronulla dudes were out there. But here at last was a story that had real resonances with my own life. I was almost embarrassed to pass it around because there was a lot of secret, sacred surf stuff in it that exposed exactly what we'd been getting up to at the beach—stuff that, until now we'd managed to keep under wraps. Despite my caution about spreading the book around, its publication caused a sensation and McPhee Gribble Publishers rushed off a second print run before the year was out. Carey and Lette had flagrantly exposed contemporary beach culture and the surfie chick's role in it for all the world to see.

2

AUSSIE BEACH MOVIE

Someone who had been watching this phenomenon with delight was Margaret Kelly. In the late 1970s she had been living at Whale Beach, north of Sydney, and working as a television series writer. Her young sons were both surfers and it had struck her that there was no real Australian beach movie. Sure, there had been 8-mm and 16-mm surfing documentaries that were screened in surf clubs and assorted halls to an audience predominantly made up of boys bonging on but never a successful feature film. *Crystal Voyager* and *Morning of the Earth* might have been feature length, they were still basically documentaries, following real life surfers on their various safaris. Christopher Fraser had tried his hand at it in 1977 with *Summer City* but, apart from providing Mel Gibson with his first screen role, the flick did little to connect with the wider public. Two years later Albie Thoms gave it a go with *Palm Beach* starring Bryan Brown and Nat Young but again it failed to make a big impact. It seemed extraordinary that no one had succeeded in spinning a fictional cinematic narrative around a beach setting, considering that the majority of Australians lived within a short distance of the coast. So Kelly started getting some ideas together for a script centred on beach life by eavesdropping on her sons and their buddies for dialogue.

During this time she was also helping out at the Shopfront Theatre for Young People in the south Sydney suburb of Carlton, reading scripts written by aspiring young writers. At one of these Saturday workshops teenagers Gabrielle Carey and Kathy Lette rocked up with an exercise book full of hand-written stories. 'They were original short stories that they wrote about being surfie chicks', Kelly recalled. 'I thought they were really great. They showed all the sort of fresh talent, plus they'd been there and they'd actually researched it. I just started working with them on their stories.'[7] Carey and Lette called their collection *Puberty Blues* and, sensing something truly original, Kelly took out an option to write a feature film based on them and raised some development funding from the Australian Film Commission. 'Every word of that script was workshopped with us first', recalled Lette who had run away from home the day after her sixteenth birthday and was being nurtured by Carey's parents while she and Gabrielle tried to find a publisher for their book. 'If it hadn't been for Gabrielle's parents being so liberal, we wouldn't have read the *National Times*, seen Anne Summers' bi-line, sent her the manuscript, which she then sent onto McPhee Gribble', said Lette explaining that their story had been turned down by all the other publishers that they'd sent it to.

While the young writers worked with a literary editor, Kelly concentrated on creating a film narrative from their episodic tales. She had also decided that she wanted to produce and this was the project on which she would cut her teeth. 'I realised that it was a bit of a minefield and I needed to take on a co-producer', she said, explaining why she approached Joan Long, then President of the Australian Writer's Guild and a highly regarded figure in the film industry. Long had directed two documentaries exploring Australia's early film days: *The Pictures That Moved: Australian Cinema 1896 – 1920* and *The Passionate Industry*. She had written the successful feature film *Caddie* about a strong-willed woman struggling to bring up two children in the late 1920s and early 1930s and had also written and produced *The Picture Show Man,* again set in the 1920s, centring on a showman who brings movies to small country towns. These films dealt with a world long since past and while they might have depicted the lives of Aussie battlers during the Depression, they did so at a good arm's length through sepia tinted glasses.

Since the success of Peter Weir's *Picnic at Hanging Rock* in 1975 there had been a spate of such 'picturesque period' films emerging from the burgeoning Australian film industry. In their book *The Screening of Australia: Anatomy of a National Cinema,* Susan Dermody and Elizabeth Jacka explain that while

> not necessarily the largest nor the most commercially successful group ... these films have tended to be the most 'citable', the ones deemed worthy of international showcasing and that have earned honourable mention, if not glory, for Australia as a fledgling film culture.[8]

Beresford's Victorian coming of age story, *The Getting of Wisdom,* and his moving patriotic work, *Breaker Morant,* set in 1901 during the Boer War are another two examples. While *Breaker,* like Weir's *Gallipoli,* celebrated the downfall of the heroic Aussie male overseas, *Wisdom,* like Gillian Armstrong's *My Brilliant Career,* focused on the blossoming of the local lass at home. All four films drew upon real life events and their historical contexts were replicated with great authenticity. They were costume dramas with the blokes in uniform and the sheilas in corsets. The men explored their emotional frontiers in wartime while the women charted theirs in intimate journals on the home front. And to further accentuate their similarities both *Wisdom* and *Brilliant* were based on autobiographical novels written by women under male pseudonyms in the early part of last century, Henry Handel Richardson (*Wisdom*) and Miles Franklin (*Brilliant*).

But audiences began wondering about the relevance of all this looking back. Often it gave them a warm inner glow and a sense of pride about where they'd come from but it was a mythologised representation and had little to say about contemporary Australia. In his book, *Australian National Cinema*, Tom O'Regan articulates this mood:

> Critic after critic, filmmaker after filmmaker maintained that what Australian culture needed was contemporary representations, not nostalgia films set in a mythic past. Australians needed to be resituated within their own culture and history with new and more relevant symbols than that of the Australian legend, mateship and the Aussie battler.[9]

Puberty Blues was a far cry from all those picturesque period films which dripped sentimentality and nostalgia. It was about a group of people at the very bottom of the social food chain—contemporary teenage girls. While Joan Long, having brought up a daughter, had experience of young girls, she knew very little of the species of girl depicted in this story. Nevertheless, she was at heart a feminist and sympathised with the story so she agreed to co-produce the film. However, according to Kelly, the first thing she wanted to do after committing to the project was change the title. She also tried to tone down some of the more hard-core language but, realising that this authenticity was the key to the story's uniqueness, Kelly stuck by the original material.

Meanwhile, Carey and Lette were on the publicity bandwagon for their book, reinforcing every raunchy word they had written. They even appeared on television singing ditties with quaint lyrics like:

> Well I had spoof all over my jeans.
> My Mother asked me if I dropped my ice cream.
> I said, No Mama,
> I'm a big girl now (she won't believe me, no she won't believe me)
> No Mama, I've turned thirteen.[10]

According to Kelly, this sort of exposure gave Joan Long conniptions:

> The girls, as everybody called them, were really quite outrageous. They loved shocking people and so they were doing all these interviews and saying all these outrageous things as we were about to make the film and Joan was just freaking out saying, 'Oh my God, somebody's got to talk to them. We'll never get the film made. People are just going to hate this'. She did talk to them a few times and said, 'Can you tone it down?'

Little did she realise that the girls were building the audience for the film as well as the book with every scandalous statement they made.

Long would eventually have to concede that her fears about the title, the language and the public's taste were unfounded but not before she had given Kelly, in particular, a good dose of her own diametrically opposed sensibility. For a start, she was a passionate film lover and Kelly thought she looked down on people who worked in television. It cut no ice for Long that for over a decade Kelly had been writing for popular TV series like *Homicide* and *Division 4*, nor that she had won a Logie Award for Best Television Script and an Awgie Award for Best TV Drama Script for the six part series *Pig In A Poke*, co-written with her then partner, John Dingwell. The two women's working methods were very different and their relationship soon became strained but Long couldn't get rid of Kelly: 'I think she would've if she could've but it was my project and I actually had the option on the rights and they weren't signed over until the film was being made. So she had to work with me.' Instead of beating her head against Kelly's brick wall, Long turned her attention to raising the budget.

Getting enough money to make a full-length feature film about teenage surfie chicks and their sexist boyfriends was a challenge. Fortunately this was the dawning of a tax incentive system known as 10BA, which was introduced in October 1980 after a 12-month production drought. A contemporary newspaper article reveals that only six features had been made during that year which, compared with the previous three years when between sixteen and twenty films had been completed annually, was a worrying figure.[11] Now, with the announcement of this cash cow, there were more than twenty productions planned for 1981, each set to take a dip into the $30 million pool of government and private investment. As it transpired, a full $50 million was made available in the first year of the 10BA scheme, money that all hinged on a films' Australian content. The film critic Geraldine Pascall wrote that there was an onus on filmmakers

> to ensure that this windfall is used for films of quality and merit, commercial productions that appeal to a wide audience and that it does not become the lucrative plaything

> of the tax rip-off industry or of film hustlers, home-grown or imported.[12]

Of course, 10BA is now remembered for producing a climate in which exactly this type of exploitation occurred. With a 150% tax concession on offer, people invested in the industry in their droves resulting in a legacy of notoriously dodgy films.

Puberty Blues, however, had its own special type of integrity. There were no glaring contrivances in the story; it was all based on fact and it certainly had wide commercial appeal, judging by the response to the book which was still being pumped out to satisfy demand and was reprinted five times in just two years. The producers had started raising the money for the film under the old tax system with an investment from the Australian Film Commission of just less than 50%. They cobbled together the rest of the $843,000 budget from about 56 different investors including little syndicates of people who each put in a thousand dollars. 'It was a very big job raising money for the film and looking after all the investors, with all the legal work and enquiries to handle', Long revealed at the time.

> Then there was an election promise [for tax concessions] by the Minister for Home Affairs, Bob Elliott, and everyone believed that if the Liberals got in on October 18, 1980, they would honour their promise. We found investments were coming a lot more quickly after that...[13]

What really got the investors excited, however, was the news that Beresford wanted to direct the film. He had spotted the book in a shop window whilst waiting for a bus in North Sydney and went in to buy it. By the time he had reached his destination he knew he wanted to make a film of it. Here was a slice of life that had never been represented on the screen before and, with its

Director Bruce Beresford with the surfie chicks

panoramic beach setting, one that had great cinematic potential. He tracked down the producers and wrote them a letter saying that he was keen. Long and Kelly had originally offered the job to Gillian Armstrong who had just made her stunning debut, *My Brilliant Career*, but she turned it down, signing up instead for another colourful teen movie slated for production that same year called *Star Struck*.

While the producers may have preferred a female at the helm of their feminist film, they certainly weren't going to turn down a director of Beresford's calibre. *Breaker Morant* had broken box office records in Australia and had just been screened in competition at the Cannes Film Festival, winning its star, Jack Thompson, a special Best Supporting Actor award. Besides, Beresford had some credentials directing young women, too. *The Getting of Wisdom*, which had screened at Cannes in the 1978 Director's Fortnight showcase, featured a cast of teenage schoolgirls. It was also a feminist film with a lesbian identity at its heart and while the relationship between Debbie and Sue may not have been a lesbian one it was certainly something extra special. Joan Long had no hesitation in accepting Beresford's offer. As she told film critic David Stratton:

Nell Schofield as Debbie

> I felt you could trust Bruce with all aspects of a film, because his judgement is so good. He's good at casting, script assessment, editing, everything; he's a film person—he didn't come up from television—and he's a director after my own heart.[14]

With Beresford on board, Long and Kelly were able to secure the last of the money they needed to make the film and finalised a deal enabling them to go into production. There was, however, one supremely ironic moment that made the film teeter just before shooting began. Joan Long, the figurehead of this film about puberty, was going through menopause. 'Consequently her moods were incredibly irrational', revealed Kelly.

> She had the most amazing mood swings and no one knew why, including me. Because all she'd ever say to me was 'It's women's troubles'. I didn't know what it was. I mean, that covers a big range. But one day she just abused the shit out of Bruce, just out of the blue. She just lost it over nothing. And he got up and left and flew to the Gold Coast. We were without a movie.

The producers had raised the last of their money on the condition that Beresford direct and it was imperative that they get him back.

> I had to track Bruce down and give his number to Joan and say you have to get him back. And she did. I don't know what she said, but he came back onto the project. It was very touch and go.

Meanwhile I was starting to think twice about pursuing a career in acting. My encounters with professional actors revealed that most of them seemed to spend a large percentage of their time unemployed. I had finished my HSC, John Lennon had been assassinated and from where I stood the future looked rather pear-shaped. Then I got a call asking if I'd be interested in auditioning for *Puberty Blues*. As it turned out, Margaret Kelly's son knew that I was a keen surfie chick and had suggested me to his mother. Beresford had been scouring the country for the part of Debbie but nobody wanted to do it, at least that's what he said.[15] Looking back, I can see why but at the time I was game for anything.

In the book, Debbie and Sue are just thirteen, a fact that makes the story particularly confronting given that they and their friends are loosing their virginity left right and centre. But as with *Fast Times at Ridgemont High,* Amy Heckerling's early 1980s cult teen flick from the States, the cast had to be at least sixteen to comply with legal and union regulations (in Heckerling's case, this meant relegating the considerable talents of one underage actor called Nicholas Cage to a blink-and-you'll-miss-it role). Determined that the film reach its target teen audience, the producers met with representatives from the Film Censorship Board in pre-production to discuss the parameters for an M rating that would allow teenagers to see it. They were advised not to depict any instructional drug taking and above all, not to mention the age of any of the characters. The 'teenage' cast of *Puberty Blues* ranged in age from sixteen to twenty-five, a fact that irked some critics. Evan Williams wrote:

> This is supposed to be a film about puberty, yet for reasons that are obvious enough, the characters are all played by teenagers—and strikingly healthy and well developed ones at that. It would have been difficult, no doubt, to find a cast of

> authentically pubescent young actors, but even if such a cast had been found, the story is so explicit and insistent in its references to menstrual and populative difficulties that questions of taste would soon have intervened. The result, of necessity, is a compromise.[16]

The eldest cast member was Tony Hughes (Danny) who lied about his age (he was twenty-five), but at least he could surf. None of the other male actors could. They all had stand-ins for their surfing shots. Of the others, Geoff Rhoe (Garry) was twenty while Jay Hackett (Bruce) and Ned Lander (Strach) were both nineteen. I was seventeen and my co-star, Jadranka Capelja, was the youngest at just sixteen.

Jad was about to go into fourth form (year 10) and had already attended about eight casting sessions for the part of Sue Knight. She was there on the casting couch when I first met her, awaiting some kind of decision. Jad was a gorgeous girl who had been born in Novisaard, near Belgrade, in what was then Yugoslavia and emigrated to Australia when she was just six. While she'd had plenty of experience in the art of acting with local Sydney theatre groups, she had little knowledge of surf culture and knew nothing whatsoever of the book before auditioning. Jadranka, whose name coincidentally translates as 'the sea', was again everything I was not – beautiful, blonde and naïve. Together we made a special pair. She laughed at my silly jokes and made me feel in command of every situation, starting off with the confronting screen test. With her by my side I knew I could do this thing. We could be comrades in bikinis, enduring with some modicum of dignity the hideous initiation ceremonies that the script held in store for us.

As we waited for our turn in front of the camera I filled Jad in on my surfing background. Suddenly Beresford was all ears, 'Can you surf?' he asked excitedly. 'Sure', I replied, wondering why he didn't already know. I could see the finale of the film begin to take shape right there and then in his mind. Years later in the interview that he and I did for the DVD he says he was always looking for a girl who could surf as well as act but I think he might have been rewriting history. At the end of the film Debbie and Sue try their hand at surfing. The script described a scene in which the pair muck about in the water and have a ball, just like they do in the book. Debbie says:

> I knelt twice. Sue giggled so much she couldn't even make it to shore lying down. We didn't venture very far out. If I did catch a big wave I just clutched the sides of our board and screamed all the way in. It was unreal fun.[17]

And this was the essence of the penultimate scene in the film script. Beresford, however, wisely utilised my surfing ability to create a thrilling, if implausible, finale. No-one could actually surf that well on the very first attempt but when Debbie does the film is elevated to an almost mythic dimension.

The newspapers reported that I landed the part over four hundred and ninety other girls. Call it publicity hype or fact; the part was crying out for someone exactly like little old me. I know I had a strange feeling of destiny from that very first phone call and it was vindicated within a week. My future was spread out before me like so many lines in the sand. I was going to be an actress, just as I had predicted all those years ago. In subsequent interviews I revealed that I 'drank champagne for weeks' after the winning the role and that 'my Dad started to cry when I told him I had the part. He was just so happy.'[18] I suspect he hadn't read the book. People would ask me if I'd ever had any acting experience before and I'd reply that there was always lots of drama at home. In reality though, I had been in front of the cameras on several occasions, the first being at the age of six months as a model for a magazine advertisement for the British Egg Marketing board. As an advertiser, my father had sent me out to earn my keep from a very early age. The only movie role I'd ever had before was when I was eight, playing a non-speaking part in a lost Australian period piece called *David and Pywaket*, in which the maid says to me: 'Little girls should be seen and not heard.' I never did pay any heed to that.

Filming for *Puberty Blues* started on 17 January 1981 and I remember the thrill of being picked up at 5am for the 40km drive south to Cronulla. The first scene we shot was the one with Debbie and Sue playing space invaders – a very 1970s game that I had been obsessed with myself. Years later, in 2003, the Comedy Channel picked up on this scene for its film promos, pre-empting their screenings with a clip overlaid with the following tantalising tease: 'Back when space invaders were hot and girls wore ugly leotards...' It does indeed seem like a very long time ago. As Debbie shoots down icons on the screen she reveals to Sue that there's something wrong with her. 'He couldn't get it in' she confides. Imagine: day one and there I am surrounded by a bunch of strangers all beaming in on this private and highly personal revelation. It was a case of in at the deep end. But Beresford was so endearing, just like a big kid himself, that I totally trusted his judgement and gave myself over into his hands.

3

DICKHEADLAND

As the filmmakers knew only too well, if a film about Australian surf culture was going to succeed, it had to be big, bright and beautiful to hook audiences in and reflect the expansiveness of the beach. So the decision was made by Beresford and McAlpine to shoot in widescreen with an anamorphic lens, the same lens that produced the famous 'Cinemascope' and 'Panavision' effects. What anamorphic essentially does is squeeze a wide scene through the camera on to the film at a ratio of 1:2. When projected the film is then unsqueezed to become twice as wide. The result is a panoramic picture captured on conventional film stock. McAlpine had used anamorphic on *Barry McKenzie Holds His Own* and to this day still swears by it. 'The format tells the audience that they are watching a movie not a TV special…' he says,

> But the truth is I love it. It's such a wonderful wide stage to work on, like an opera theatre. The screen rolls wider and the audience sees something spectacular. There's a subconscious 'wow' factor. I've used it on most of the films I have done. It's a bit of a trade mark.[19]

The opening sequence of the film is a celebration of the format, capturing the mood of a blisteringly hot Sydney summer day brilliantly. We see an impossibly crowded beach. Colourful bodies seethe around the shoreline and bob about in the breakers. We are looking down on South Cronulla. As we discover in just a moment, via Debbie's narration, this part of the beach is known as 'Dickheadland'. It was Beresford's idea to use direct readings from the book to reinforce Kelly's screenplay as he felt there were classic lines that could not be spoken as dialogue. Kelly initially resisted this idea feeling that it revealed a weakness in the script but Beresford held the reins and the narration stayed. Using Debbie's first person, past tense voice-over throughout the film also gives it a retrospective tone. The character is looking back on the action from a safe distance, often with humour, drawing the audience in to her now much wiser viewpoint.

It was also Beresford's idea to use music by Split Enz. In the book there are references to heavier groups like T-Rex, Deep Purple and Led Zepplin but this popular New Zealand band would, he thought, be more suitable. The producers agreed – it would certainly be cheaper – but they insisted that the songs be sung by a woman. After all, this was a film about women, or rather girls, and life as seen from their point of view. So the theme song was written by Split Enz lead singer Tim Finn and sung (uncredited) by his compatriot, Sharon O'Neill.

The very sound of this waltz-like refrain sends spasms through my gut. Having been taunted by people singing it to me for the past twenty-three years, it has an uncanny ability to induce a physical reaction. An Internet Movie Data Base user noted in a summary of the film that: 'Embarrassing-skeletons-in-the-closet awards must go to Tim Finn for writing the title song, and Les Gock who was also responsible for some of the music.'[20] I can only agree. However, the fact that people can still reel it off (a sixteen-year-old girl sang it to me only yesterday) proves that it's nothing if not catchy.

In the next shot we are introduced to our protagonists, Debbie and Sue, striking out on their hour-long journey up the beach's social ladder.[21] It's a punishing walk, especially in the height of summer. As Sue later says at the end of it: 'Deadset, we nearly melted our tits off getting here', a corker of a line and one held dear by many. Debbie is wearing a light baby (puberty) blue top while Sue, the more feminine of the pair, is wearing a pink sarong. The theme's chorus kicks in:

> Pu-ber-ty Blues, it's you and me against the world...

This lyric sets up the idea that these two girls are about to take on something big and indeed they are. It might not be the entire world but it is a particular microcosm, and one that they have to break out of in order to see that a bigger world exists. A freckly redhead (Tina Robinson), whose pale body is accentuated by her orange bikini, spots the girls and calls out to them by name. Sue registers and nudges Debbie as if to find out how she should respond. Debbie, obviously the leader of the two, dismisses the girl with a single word: 'moll'. A moll, as we learn from the book is 'an easy root'—to root, of course, meaning to have sexual intercourse.[22] Such a derisive description comes as a shock from one so apparently innocent and it sets the tone for the sort of coarse language to come.

We meet this spurned redhead again and follow her sad fate throughout the film for she is the unfortunate Freda, a girl whose main crime was to have been born ugly. Beresford wanted to cast a fat girl in this role but Kelly, being a large woman, rejected the idea:

> I said to Bruce, why does every nerd have to be fat? Let's give her red hair but Joan said 'No!', because she had red hair. Still, we got Tina. She had red hair and freckles and didn't have a tan.

This is the first interaction the girls have with anyone in the film and it represents a marker for the journey that they are on. We will revisit this first encounter with Freda in an echoing shot at the very end when Debbie and Sue see her in a whole new light. But for now she is simply a 'moll', a permanent fixture of 'Dickheadland', and someone to be avoided at all costs.

The camera zooms in on a surfer riding a wave. It continues to pans past him to pinpoint the girls' destination, way off at the northern end of the beach near the smoke stacks of the Kurnell oil refinery just visible on the horizon. Don McAlpine is given his full screen credit here and film buffs may be reminded of another great Australian cinematographer, Frank Hurley, who captured these very same sand hills in *Forty Thousand Horsemen,* Charles Chauvel's 1940 classic film about the First World War.[23]

Back at the contemporary chick flick, Debbie and Sue claim a spot and pull out their towels as the camera continues tracking up to reveal a group of girls nearby. One of them, Tracey (Sandy Paul) is smoking. She alerts the other two, Vicki (Joanne Olsen) and Kim (Julie Medana), to the newcomers moving in on their turf and they call them derisive names like 'crawlers' and 'brown-noses'. Debbie and Sue ignore their taunts. They are moving in on this territory and nothing will stop them.

They focus on the surfers in front of them including Danny (Tony Hughes), another freckly redhead, incidentally, but cool because he's a surfie. All the surfing in the film is presented in slow motion to distinguish it as something sacred and lyrical, a far cry from the mundane, pedestrian world onshore. Our bosom buddies now recognise Cheryl (Leanda Brett) cantering up the beach bareback on her white horse. In the book all the girls ride. Debbie explains that her 'horse, Misty had gone lame. Sue didn't have one but we always doubled.'[24] In the film, Cheryl is the only one who has a horse although we do see Tracy mounted on one at the surfie funeral further down the track. The reason why Cheryl is so often seen astride her trusty stead is never spelt out in the film. However, in the book, it's there in black and white: 'It was well known a girl was a better root if she rode a horse.'[25] Cheryl, the root rat, rides close by the 'crawlers' and her horse kicks sand all over them. The film cuts immediately to a stunning low angle wide shot, worthy of being airbrushed on the side of a panel van, of the panoramic beach while up above puffy white clouds float in an electric blue sky. Its pure crisp colour, the essence of an Australian beach in summer. In just three and a half minutes, perfect pop song duration, the scene has been set for our surfie saga.

4

OUT OF BOUNDS

In the Greenhills Gang, being cool means being bad and this involves pushing boundaries. Both the book and the film make a point about territory and how entering forbidden zones is all part of these teenage girls' rite of passage. They no longer feel at home in their family circles. The beach and school are now where it's at and the school bus provides the perfect transitional place for Debbie and Sue to make their next move on Gangland—specifically, the back of the bus. Greenhills Gang-girl Cheryl intervenes, relegating the interlopers to a seat up the front, another Dickheadland of sorts. Our 'crawlers' try to assert themselves by calling Cheryl names. Sue starts off with 'Bitch-face' and Debbie chimes in with 'box-tosser', a term not found in the book but offered up by Beresford during rehearsals.[26] It is Sue who has the final say with, 'fish-face moll'; a description, incidentally, often hurled my way by some of my more intimate friends who have only recently cottoned on to the film's outrageous turns of phrase.

Further classic 1970s lingo follows when the girls eye off their dream boys. For Debbie, it's Garry (Jeff Rhoe): 'What a spunk' she swoons. For Sue it's Cheryl's boyfriend, Danny: 'What a deadset doll!' But coveting these guys comes with a penalty and Cheryl extracts it by hurling her half-sucked orange at the back of Deb's head. Deb retaliates and it's on. The two go at each other in the aisle and the Gang eggs them on. Finally the bus driver slams on the breaks and they go flying down the aisle. It looks painful, and it was. The camera was bolted low on the floor for this shot and I came thumping down onto it with Leander on top of me. My head ached for days. Suppressing the pain, we continued fighting, pulling each other hard by the pigtails. At this point Deb and Cheryl are equals. It's a major victory for the girl who, only a few minutes ago was labelled a 'crawler'. Things are looking up.

A large part of the story focuses on the world of school but finding one in which to shoot was not an easy task. The reputation of Carey and Lette's book had made it extremely difficult to secure a location in the Sutherland Shire, as Kelly revealed at the time:

> The schools are most antagonistic because they think the authors have given Sylvania High, in particular, a very bad name... none of the schools in that area wanted to know about us.[27]

The producers went through the Education Department and finally arrived at a compromise: they could film in a school as long as it was on the city side of the Cooks River just a few kilometres west of Sylvania Waters. The actual school used in the film, as I was reminded just the other week by a bloke who remembered being in the assembly scenes as a kid, was James Cook Boys High in Kogarah. It was a badge of honour for him and a bit of infamy, no doubt, for the school itself.

From the primal behaviour on the bus we cut to a static aerial shot looking down on a hall full of silent students mid-exam. A long tracking shot takes us past studious teenagers, including our friend Freda the 'moll', to the back of the hall which, like the back of the bus, is where we find the Greenhills Gang. In a neat montage we see that they're up to no good. Debbie and Sue are also cheating and find themselves in the powerful position of being able to help their dreamboats, Garry and Danny. They do so eagerly, crossing yet another boundary between their status as 'dickheads' and their aim to be part of the 'in' crowd. But one of the teachers spots them. They're busted!

How they deal with this is a major test for the novices. In the Principal's office, Mr Bishop (Charles 'Bud' Tingwell) confronts the hangdog quartet lined up in front of him with the critical question: 'Who else was involved?' It's a pivotal moment for the young 'crawlers' and when confronted by name, Deborah has no hesitation in covering up; 'Nobody, Sir' she says, pulling her skirt down over the writing on her thigh, a method of cheating she has copied from Cheryl. Susan also replies in the negative. They have protected the other cheats and will take the rap for all of them with two weeks worth of detention.

Being in trouble is what the Greenhills Gang is all about. By defying adult authority our girls are inching ever closer to their goal. Suddenly they are worth speaking to. Even Tracy is calling to them across the asphalt. They're being summoned by the top surfie chick! An aerial shot looks down on huge yellow letters that read 'Out of Bounds'. This is the desired territory. Debbie and Sue can hardly hide their excitement at being invited into it. Vicki asks: 'Did you dob?' 'No Way' responds Deb, thrilled at how her discretion is paying such quick dividends. 'Deadset?' asks Tracy. 'Deadset' Sue assures her. Have they passed the test? Tracy looks at Cheryl who seals their fate: 'Wanna come down the dunnies for a smoke?'

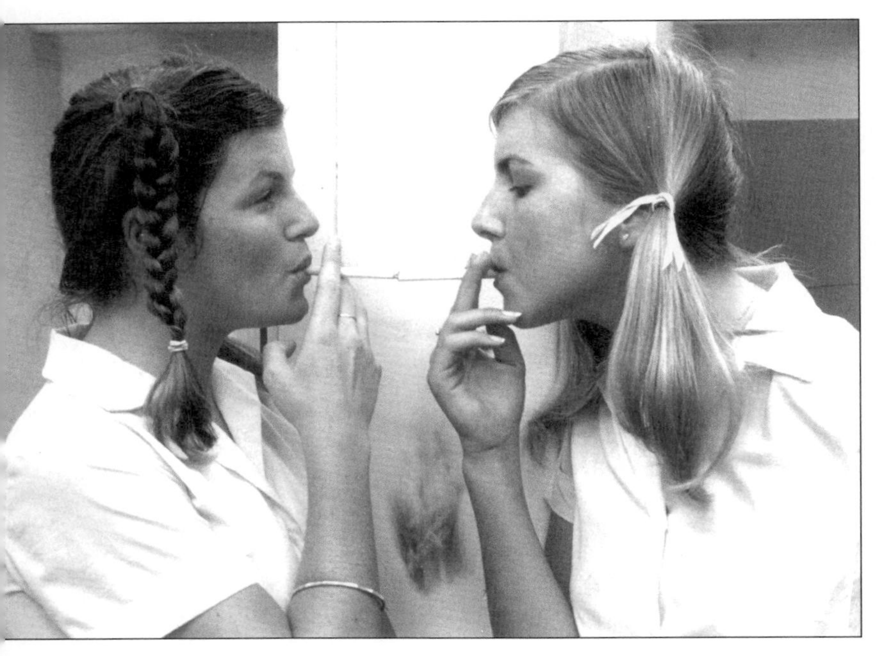

The first rite of initiation

Our crawlers are in. They've just graduated into the surfie gang and are about to be inducted into its first ritual—smoking. As if to celebrate their victory, the theme tune starts up as they all strut into the toilet block. Juniors scatter before the oncoming six-pack. Tracy bangs on a toilet door and evicts a girl. This is Beresford's own daughter Cordelia, now an award-winning filmmaker herself, who is bullied into standing guard outside while the gang claims another territory. A red lighter ignites Debbie's cigarette and she turns to Sue who lights her own ciggie off it. Our initiates are joined by the tips of their cigarettes in a shared moment of intimacy.

In the 1970s there were no advertising campaigns aimed at educating the public about the dangers of smoking. It took until 1990 for the Federal government to address the issue through television and cinema advertisements and only in 1992 did it place a blanket ban on tobacco advertising.[28] Back then we were deluged by alluring ads featuring fabulous looking people riding horses at altitude and blissfully smoking beneath waterfalls. Peter Weir has a great time sending up these images in the opening sequence of *The Cars That Ate Paris* (1974) when a cool dude in his Datsun 1600 convertible picks up his carefree babe for spin in the country and a luxurious puff on an Alpine.

Smokin' down the dunnies

At Sydney High we would do pretty much exactly what the *Puberty Blues* characters are doing. Some of my friends were so addicted to nicotine that they would have to excuse themselves from class and rush off to the toilets for a quick drag. There were no patches back in those days and quit lines were still way off in the future. Just like baking yourself to a crisp on the beach was *de rigueur* to get that desired tan, smoking was simply what you did if you were a fashion conscious person. Under-aged school kids doing it furtively in the unhygienic environment of the toilet block was all part of the equation.

Debbie and Sue are gasping discreetly, trying not to let on that this initiation is anything but a joyride, when the junior announces that the teacher's coming. A frantic scramble follows as the girls dump their butts into the overhead cisterns, already home to several floating remnants. Ignorant of this part of the ritual, Deb chucks her butt down the toilet but the recalcitrant object swirls about the bowl, refusing to go down the S-bend. We will see many toilets throughout the film. It's almost an obsession. They represent a private space, a place for waste, a place of triumph and, if you like, a direct link to the beach where the ocean outfall connects it to the sea.

The frequent references to toilets throughout the film caught the eye of Daniel Mudie Cunningham, a teacher of film art and design theory who did his doctoral thesis on 'White Trash Aesthetics' which he believes inform the film. He too grew up in the Sutherland Shire, the Bible Belt of south Sydney and, like Debbie, was sent to Church Fellowship by his parents. 'It's so middle class but you scratch beneath the surface and it's just so much trash. There seems to be something rotten at its core', he explained. 'There's this really strong trash culture operating within the Shire, totally in contrast to the surface of it, which is the religious factor.'[29]

Sue's upbringing is less inclined towards Christianity. Her mother (Rowena Wallace) wears sarongs and eats salads. Perhaps she's a bit of a hippie? But home is of no consequence to either of the girls. The world of their peers has superseded it. As the book explains: '...the surfie gang had a big, more important family of its own'.[30] We see Deb and Sue running along the street to catch up with Tracy and Cheryl who is once again straddling her white steed.

Down at the paddock, Debbie learns that Bruce Board (Jay Hackett) has his eyes on her. She is thrilled to bits. So is Sue on her behalf, 'Isn't it perf?' she enthuses. Deb swoons then asks comically, 'Who is he?' The idea of a boy from the Greenhills Gang actually fancying her is like a dream come true. It doesn't matter who he is. She is now a desirable commodity. For these girls, identity is intricately linked with boys. Girls are acknowledged as inferior and can only validate their existence in relation to boys. On hearing that this Bruce character works for his father and has his own panel van Deb gets anxious. A panel van is a major status symbol. Otherwise known as a 'shaggin' wagon', these vehicles are synonymous with sex. 'Do I look alright?' she asks to which Tracy replies 'rootable'. What more could a girl ask for?

In a high angle shot the girls plunge into the dark undergrowth of the paddock where Debbie's first uncomfortable encounter with the opposite sex is about to occur. A long low tracking shot follows them as they walk deeper into what looks like a jungle. This is a much more benign place than the beach, with lots of protection from the beating sun.

The rest of the Gang is sprawled around their shady territory and Bruce clocks Debbie through his big rose-coloured sunnies. He takes them off to get a better look. He hasn't seen her properly before yet she is the one he's chosen from afar. Debbie doesn't even know who she's looking for and has to ask. Meanwhile, Danny has spotted Sue, all wide-eyed and naïve, chewing away on her gum. Like the little kid that she is, Sue blows a big green bubble. Danny smiles at the sight of it and Sue catches his eye. The bubble bursts and Sue smiles shyly back at him. Danny will be the one to burst Sue's bubble, so to speak, and claim her virginity in the not too distant future. But for now he's still giving Cheryl love bites 'all over'. Tracy, the matchmaker, goes to work introducing Debbie to Bruce. The other blokes in the Gang goad him on and he crudely removes his gum to give Debbie a solid smooch. Being the centre of attention in a situation like this is not the most romantic thing a girl could imagine and the embarrassment is clear on Debbie's face. Bruce pops his chewy back in his mouth then asks Deb if she'll 'go round' with him. How could she refuse such a tempting offer? Bruce extracts his gum for one more rough kiss to howls of delight from the Gang. The only one not participating in this ritual is Garry. He's perched up in a tree watching the proceedings with calm detachment. Does he disapprove of this pairing? Could he have a soft spot for Debbie himself? Or is he, as has been suggested, in fact gay?[31] From a high angle perspective, not unlike Garry's own, we see Bruce usher Debbie off.

So Debbie undergoes the second rite of passage and secures herself a boyfriend. What this means in the context of this particular Gang is demonstrated when, after coming to the end of the hour-long march up the beach, Debbie sets about folding

Bruce's clothes. This is the role of a surfie chick. It's what all the crawling, brownnosing and sucking up has been about. Surfie chicks are expected to idolize their boyfriends and Debbie dutifully does this, admiring Bruce (or rather, a body double) carve up a wave. Then she and the rest of the gang settle down to what for girls is the serious business of the beach—sunbaking. There's a slightly pervy quality to this montage which was picked up by the critic Sandra Hall who wrote '... at odds with the script's feminist tone is the camera's voyeuristic propensity for lingering on bare bodies.'[32] Another critic, Elizabeth Riddell, also commented on this tendency: 'the camera lingers on those lovely out-of-uniform legs and arms, not to mention tops and bottoms.'[33] When I watch this scene I'm immediately taken back to the most painful time in the entire shoot. I remember almost crying with the discomfort of it. Judy Lovell, the lovely make-up artist was eternally sympathetic but was under strict instructions to oil us up for a good fry. You can see us turning puce before your very eyes.

Kathy Lette has said that she used to sunbake with a customised piece of cut-out cardboard on her stomach so that she had her boyfriend's name tattooed by the sun onto her skin, joking that one day she'll have a melanoma named 'Bruce'.[34] Picador picked up on this detail for the front cover of the 2002 edition of *Puberty Blues* which features an image of a sandy suntanned belly with 'BRUCE' stencilled on the flesh above a pink bikini bottom. The name sits just next to a blue condom tucked into the bikini band. Sun, sand and sex, the essence of this 'Great Australian Classic'.[35]

This edition also includes a pair of forewords by the unlikely double act of Australian expats Germaine Greer and Kylie Minogue. Lette herself asked the pair for a contribution: 'I felt that was appropriate—stereophonic Aussie goddesses!' The pop star recalls 'devouring' the book:

> I was about thirteen, alone in my bedroom with the door firmly shut... I was whisked into a world of boys, the beach and best friends. Of pimples, periods and panel vans. Such things were important to know and I was fascinated. The honesty of the story made it hysterical and terrifying at the same time. The language was identifiable and spoke volumes through its simplicity.[36]

Greer, on the other hand, adopts the role of a responsible adult in her foreword: '*Puberty Blues* is a profoundly moral story which should chill the marrow of parents of today's thirteen-year-olds.'

A vast generation gap is evident here. The pop princess relishes the memory of reading the book while the feminist academic sees it as a cautionary tale. Commenting on the contemporary relevance of the story Greer writes:

> *Puberty Blues* is not only a period piece, nor is its colour merely local. The tribal society into which Debbie and Sue are so painfully and destructively inducted still rules in the dead reaches of suburbia... The boredom that so terrorised Debbie and Sue has deepened into total inertia and deep silence...[37]

The inclusion of forewords by these two high profile international figures gives added weight to the enduring significance of the book. While neither references the film, it too is a potent social document of this particular sub-culture, visually capturing its mores.

Back in melanomaland, Deb is awakened from the bake-off when Bruce wrings water onto her burning face and accuses her of not watching his surfing prowess. Her entire life should now be devoted to him. She has to back pedal fast to redeem herself. One after the other, she meets his requests: a towel, a cigarette… she even offers to go to the shop and get him and his mates a ridiculously long list of junk food—Chiko Rolls, those disgusting deep fried fat spring rolls, chocolate thick shakes, dim sims. We hear another voice over from Debbie using lines from the book:

> Girls never ate in front of their boyfriends. It was unladylike to open your mouth and shove something in it. We were also busting to go to the dunny, but that was too rude for girls. Our stomachs rumbled and our bladders burst.[38]

Being a surfie chick might have been the be all and end all at Cronulla Beach but in reality it was agony. It was a form of slavery.

At least Debbie has Sue who volunteers to accompany her gal pal on the hour-long trek back down the beach and then up again—two hours in all! If their tits haven't melted off by then, then they never will. This is true friendship. In fact, theirs is the most important relationship in the whole film. At its core, this is a buddy flick, a bosom buddy flick. No matter what happens, these two have each other. As the camera cranes up to emphasise the huge distance they have to travel, a supremely deluded Debbie turns to Sue and says, 'Isn't this great?'

From this subservience, the natural progression in a Greenhills Gang relationship is sexual intercourse and Debbie's first go at it occurs at the local drive-in. To the teenagers it hardly matters what movie is playing. In the book it's Dennis Hopper's 1969 cult youth rebellion movie *Easy Rider*, but here it's the B-grade horror flick, *Thirst*. Our surfie Gang arrives just at the point where a woman or 'blood cow' is being milked from the jugular in some twisted clinic. The horror component is no accident. Impending sex is presented as a horrific prospect for our heroine as it will be again when we see her preparing for it next to a ghoulish poster for *The Rocky Horror Picture Show*. Initially the filmmakers had planned to shoot their own horror film for this particular sequence and Leslie Caron had even expressed interest in starring in it, but budget restrictions proved prohibitive. With its mind-numbing commentary and increasingly ominous soundtrack, *Thirst* provides a suitable substitute and for many, this scene is the most memorable of the entire film. It's usually the first thing people comment on when they meet me: 'Was that you in the panel van?' I'm afraid it was. And Beresford has a ball with it too, turning a very uncomfortable situation into comedy. It's this touch throughout that makes the more confronting material so accessible and the film is often labelled a comedy as a result. In the back of the panel van Debbie is submissively following Bruce's lead and removing her clothes. Glenn (Michael Shearman) and Vicki go to the shops to get some 'eats' while Danny impresses Sue with a cigarette trick. Meanwhile Bruce, now in his leopard print undies, is delving into his 'Tool Box' for a condom. He gives Debbie a dirty look for watching him put on the contraceptive and she nervously turns away. Not a word has been spoken between them but the body language says it all. Deb is huddled up at one end of the van while Bruce occupies the other edge of the frame. From outside we see Deb part the purple curtains to witness a couple going for it hammer and tongs in the next car. It does nothing to allay her fear.

'Move down' Bruce instructs. It's the first thing he's said to her in the entire scene and she obeys just as the *Thirst* soundtrack shifts into an even more spooky gear. Suddenly we cut to an extreme close-up of a hot dog. The shot gets a huge laugh whenever audiences see it, especially from the blokes. Kelly was appalled when she first saw the rushes: 'That was Bruce's little joke. That was not in the script', she revealed. 'I remember seeing that and going "Oh, you have to be kidding". He thought it was hilarious. He's got a real boy's sense of humour.'

Bruce launches himself on to Debbie again and again with disastrous results. He bangs his head on the roof and Debbie takes the blame: his inability to penetrate her is obviously her fault. Finally he abandons the attempt with barely contained rage. 'And that was the courting ceremony at Sylvania Heights, where I grew up', Debbie's voice-over tells us. 'Well, at least I was doing something on Saturday nights.'

We now cut to the Space Invaders scene mentioned earlier, the first scene in the seven-week shooting schedule. Debbie and Sue are zapping icons out of the digital galaxy and the mechanical sound of their extermination fills the air as it did in most fun parlours during the period. In Mary Callaghan's film, *Greetings from Wollongong,* made in the same year as *Puberty Blues,* there is a scene where one of the guys goes over to his mate brandishing a newspaper clipping. 'Did you know that the yearly take for a Space Invaders machine is now estimated at one hundred million dollars?' he asks incredulously. The *Puberty Blues* girls have other, more personal, things on their minds. Debbie thinks she must be deformed or, like the space invaders, some kind of mutant being.

Yet Bruce persists with her, even going so far as to meet her parents. He's impressed by Debbie's middle class home, calling it 'a fucking mansion'. Mr Vickers (Alan Cassell) overhears and is shocked rigid, illustrating what is written in the book: 'Swearing was unheard of in my house. My pocket money was fined every time I swore or "took the Lord's name in vain."'[39] Outside, Mrs Vickers sneaks a look at Bruce's panel van and sees to her horror several pin-ups of nude women. There's also a cartoon of a copulating couple with the slogan 'Things to do... TODAY'. This must surely be every parent's worst nightmare but neither is capable of doing anything about their daughter's destiny. It would appear that the parents are intimidated by their offspring's behaviour and are rendered impotent in the face of it.

Likewise, Sue's mother doesn't bat an eyelid when she walks in to her own home to find a Gang party where everyone is engaged in various states of coupling. They're also smoking marijuana but Mrs. Knight appears hip about all this deviant activity. Either that or, like all the other adults, she's completely blind to what's really going on. She certainly doesn't register the fact that Debbie is smuggling a big jar of petroleum jelly right past her. We saw a huge close up of the Gang's preferred lubricant in the previous scene, a cartoon-like shock tactic reminiscent of the shot of the hot dog. People have confessed to me that they haven't been able to look at Vaseline in quite the same way since. Nor, needless to say, have I. The authors go further in the book explaining that

> Vaseline was an essential in surfie-life. It was used to soften eyebrows before plucking, rub into surfboard rashes, pull off your randy horse and various other things... I've still got that rusty little jar of Vaseline, all these years later, full of eyebrow and pubic hair. A little something to remember my first love.[40]

A foam surfboard wedged up against the door handle and a pair of feet hanging over the end of the bed introduces Debbie's next sexual experience. Bruce is having another go at her—we can hear his grunts and her groans as the camera tracks low across the carpeted floor revealing the bouncing springs of the bed base. Once more, things aren't going well, even with the Vaseline. 'It's hurting' we hear Debbie say. Then, after a few more grunts, 'It's no use. It's too big.' This particular line is the favourite of a twenty-five-year-old journalist who came up to me recently and asked if I would please say it for him again. When I did he quickly dialled his flatmate on his mobile phone and begged me to repeat it. The things one does to appease some of the more perverted fans!

Poor Debbie. She's now convinced there is something wrong with her. Her initiation into the supposedly wonderful world of sex is not working. After school Cheryl informs her that Bruce has 'dropped' her. The explanation? 'Too tight.' First he's too big now she's too tight. Whose problem is this? Debbie deals with the humiliation by getting pissed and Sue, as always, is right there with her. Years later, Gabrielle Carey wrote an article entitled 'I'm Not As Bad As You Were, Mum' reflecting on her role as a parent of a teenage daughter.[41] In it she referred to this autobiographical first encounter with alcohol:

> Brandevino was the cheapest drink at $1.99 so, in preparation for Danny's party (where it was practically compulsory that you arrived drunk), Kathy and I went halves and bought a bottle. Then we held our noses and drank it. Late that night Danny's father delivered us to my mother, who spent the rest of the night listening to us vomit in stereo. I

Sue and Deb hit the bottle

> was thirteen; I didn't drink again until I was twenty-two. Looking back, it was a worthwhile rite of passage.

My surfie buddies and I used to 'scull' grog too before hitting the Bondi Junction disco. I remember being busted by the police in a shocking state outside the Whale Car Wash. But we kept on drinking and chundering every weekend. Getting trashed was almost mandatory for a good night out. At least we could surf it off the next day.

5

ROOTING MACHINES

In the classroom the teenagers aren't getting any wiser. All they're interested in is their sexual development, which is simply not being addressed. The book states that they 'didn't do sex in Science till third form' – exactly one year too late for these girls.[42] Sue writes a note and passes it to Deb across the aisle, recalling their earlier cheating session. Again the teacher spots them and we cut to a close up of the note which reads: 'I think Danny wants to do it. I don't want him to think I'm just a rooting machine. Do you reckon I should let him???'

'A rooting machine' intones an authorative male voice. It is the Headmaster interrogating Sue about this outrageous description of herself. He stiltedly asks the embarrassing, almost salacious question: 'Am I to presume that you are contemplating having sexual intercourse...?' Sue denies the suggestion emphatically. The Headmaster softens into a paternalistic role and sums up his generation's expectations of young girls with the following patronising statement: 'I know you'll do the right thing eventually Susan. You'll settle down, marry, raise a family.'

With this sort of adult worldview bearing down on them it's

no wonder that these girls do everything in their power to rebel, becoming mistresses of subterfuge in the process. To avoid the mundane path mapped out for them by their elders, they side with their peers in a war of defiance, submitting themselves to their own code of cool which includes everything *but* 'settling down'. They will not be the virgin brides that their mothers were. Nor, presumably, will they raise kids as blindly as their parents. At the very least, they are experiencing life, in all its feral glory. When 'Old Bishop' dismisses Sue, he tears up the incriminating note and throws it in the waste paper basket, wiping his hands of the whole sordid affair as he does so. By not addressing the issues facing these teenagers, the educators and parents leave them open to all sorts of dangers. In the very next scene we find Garry toying with idea of buying heroin. It leads us straight in to the darkest chapter of the entire film.

It is Saturday night in the local mall and Freda's approach is heralded by the usual abuse from the boys. They even bark at her indicating exactly what they think of her. Debbie's narration explains:

> If you were pimply, a migrant, or just plain ugly you couldn't get a boyfriend. If you couldn't get a boyfriend there were two options. You could be a prude or a moll. Being a prude was too boring. At least if you were a moll people knew who you were. Like Freda Cummins.

Lumping the entire migrant population in with all those who have pimples (presumably most teenagers) and those who are ugly is a frightening display of racism but this is an Anglo male supremacist culture as is about to be clearly demonstrated.

Strach offers to give Freda a lift home with Bruce and Seagull and ushers her into the notorious panel van. We see it turn off

Saturday night down at the mall

the main road onto a deserted back street and pull up near the Kurnell oil refinery twinkling with ghostly lights. Strach drags Seagull out and takes him around to the back where he and Bruce pretend to bash him up. From Freda's point of view it looks nasty but when we cut to the action we see that it's all a sham. In a monumental act of deception the boys are appealing to Freda's maternal instincts. She is expected to leap to the defence of the smallest and probably most immature of all the Gang boys, and duly does so, pleading with the brutes to leave him alone. 'I'll screw yas', she says, offering herself up as a sacrifice. 'I'll screw the lot of yas. Just stop hurting him.'

Strach pulls down the back of the van. They've got exactly what they wanted and technically they can't be accused of rape for Freda has consented to sex with all three of them. In an uncomfortably comic touch Beresford has Bruce and Seagull dive in to the back of the van simultaneously. Strach holds them back and dictates the running order. 'Me first' he points to Bruce, 'you second', then lastly to Seagull, 'and you, slops'. Hello? Slops? This is what you give to a pig:

> swill, or the refuse of the kitchen; weak or unappetising liquid or semiliquid food; a quantity of liquid carelessly spilled or splashed about; liquid mud...

These are just some of the definitions of the word in *The Macquarie Dictionary*. It's a brutal word straight from the book and one that elicits a repulsed groan from most audience members when they hear it.[43]

This is an almost unbearable scene to watch; first the deception of Freda, then her degradation to the level of swill. Kathy Lette explained in no uncertain terms what the boys that she grew up with in Cronulla were like: they 'disproved the theory of evolution', she said in her inimitable way. 'They were evolving into apes.' She went on to say that the girls, including herself, 'were nothing more than a life support system to a vagina',[44] a statement backed up by this very scene. As Seagull mopes about, bemoaning his designation to 'slops', Bruce watches Strach get stuck into Freda in the back of his van.

The gang-bang is a sordid and persistent part of Australian culture. I recently bought a copy of the magazine *Tracks—the surfers' bible* and was shocked to read an article recalling the heyday of surf 'culture' circa 1963 – 1972 when 'dropping in' on a rival in a competition was not viewed as a penalty but as something to be settled later by a sacrificial moll:

> Someone somehow got onto the PA to announce that a notorious girl from Nat's beach, the Collaroy mascot—aka The Grunter—was willing to be served up behind the dunes to satisfy the Bondi boys... It wasn't the first dirty deed done in the history of surfing but it had a public symbolism to it at a pretty major event. First it was a group of about five, then more and more went up, between 30 and 40. The perpetrators went home all over Sydney and points north and south, and ... grew pretty well as you'd expect as role models.[45]

By 2004 things had changed, as witnessed by the fate of some other sports role models whose reputations were besmirched by their alleged participation in gang bangs. In a media frenzy it was revealed that certain members of some of the country's most successful football teams were indulging in them with regularity. Germaine Greer responded by revealing that she recalled this sort of thing going on when she was a child. 'Two elements do seem to have changed', she wrote.

> There's no question that the women are stroppier. They're not embarrassed to say they agreed to sex with one man they'd only just met, or even with two, but they insist that they hadn't agreed to being brutalised, insulted or humiliated, and they want redress.[46]

Freda has no such option. In the deserted mall, Bruce's white panel van pulls up and dumps something on the sidewalk before speeding off again. It's Freda, unceremoniously deposited right back where she started. As the poor bedraggled creature leaves the frame the camera pulls focus through the shopfront to reveal a big sign that reads 'Boysworld'. It's a heavy-handed message stating the obvious but this is where these girls are trying to forge a space for themselves, in a boys' world, and it's not going to be easy. Cultural critic Meaghan Morris wrote:

> The film tries to compensate for [the] boisterous brutality by a moment of heavy pathos as the girl stands abandoned after the event. This certainly quietened the audience down, but a nasty taste of crassness lingered on for quite a while.[47]

As often happens in this film, after something dark has occurred we're suddenly thrown into the harsh light of the beach. Boys, as we have already discovered, dominate the surf while the girls occupy a more domestic space on the sand. This time, however, as we tilt up the white sand we find Debbie looking wistfully over the demarcation line towards the water. The other surfie chicks are chittering away about girly things. Cheryl informs them that it's Strach's birthday soon and she's going to get him some black Frenchies as a present. The orchestrator of the gang bang is not punished but rewarded with an implicit offer of more sex. Something is beginning to smell very fishy around the Greenhills Gang and by the sullen look on Debbie's face she is getting a strong whiff. It prompts her to test the boundaries by expressing a desire to have a go at surfing. 'Girls don't surf' squeals Vicki as if it's the most ridiculous thing she's ever heard. All the girls laugh incredulously at the concept. This is the number one rule of the Gang and anyone who defies it is looking for trouble. In 2000 Gold Coast punk band 'Blister' released an E.P. featuring a track called *'Baby Won't You Mind My Towel'* which sampled the dialogue from this very scene—a nostalgic tongue-in-cheek ode to a time when chicks indeed did not surf. Later, in 2004, Vicious Vinyl put out a video clip made up exclusively of scenes like this from the film to accompany the song 'The First Time', a remix of Mondo Rock's 1983 hit 'Come Said the Boy' – another musical nostalgia trip inextricably linked with *Pubes*.

The film now takes a surprising turn from social realism to classic beach movie mode with a comic fight between our surfie boys and the Cronulla lifesavers. According to Kelly, Beresford came into the production office one day not long before filming commenced and insisted that she write a beach fight into the script. 'Between who?' Kelly asked somewhat perplexed. 'Between the surfies and the lifesavers', he replied as if this sort of thing happened every day. Kelly now believes that he must have seen the Californian surfing film *Big Wednesday* in preparation for his own foray into the surf genre and was inspired by its beach fight.

Garry and Deb at the bar, as featured in *The First Time* video clip

The soundtrack is pure American 1960s surf frenzy guitar harking back to every *Gidget* film ever made. The scene provides us with some comic relief after the horror of the gang bang but it has drawn criticism from several reviewers such as Jim Schembri who wrote:

> Although the scene makes its point as the girls cheer their idols on in battle, the Bud Spencer / Terence Hill type fight, with salvoes of punches and blows with surfboards failing to yield one bloody nose or misplaced tooth, is too forced and

The Greenhills Gang girls rooting for their boyfriends

> silly, and upsets the incidental tone of most of the film's comedy.[48]

Nevertheless, it gets a sure fire laugh every time. As does Mrs Vickers' warning to Debbie not to sit near the aisle at the movies: 'some pusher might come along and jab you in the arm with heaven knows what', she warns. Many a parent has been convinced that one taste of heroin could turn their child into an addict for life. My own father used to say that he didn't mind what I did as long as I didn't touch the stuff. The Gang doesn't go to the cinema (they only go to drive-ins), so there is no risk of them becoming instant junkies. However, when Danny parks his car at a section of Cronulla Beach known as Wanda, Garry lights up a big fat joint and we see Debbie and Sue consuming marijuana for the first time. So far they've been initiated into ciggies, sex, alcohol, and now dope. The results are debilitating. None of them are able to make a decision yet alone act upon it. Once again, 'the olds' don't have a clue about what's going on. Later at home when Debbie bursts into uncontrollable fits of laughter, her Mum, thinking herself an expert in these matters, explains to her husband, 'it's all a part of puberty'. This is the first time we hear the word 'puberty' as part of the dialogue, but, of course, hormones have nothing to do with it; Debbie is behaving strangely because she's stoned out of her mind, something that her parents would never guess living, as they do, in a world so far removed from teenage reality.

Debbie thanks Garry for the friendship ring

From smoking pot, it's a slippery slide down into the gutter of drug abuse. This is the message that's set up in this next scene when Garry gives Debbie a friendship ring then tells her that he had 'a hit' last night. After her euphoria at receiving the love token she is shattered to learn that he is using smack. We saw him hankering after the stuff at the mall but here is his first hand admission that 'it's really good, Deb, it's unreal'. It's a tussle of emotions between the ring and

Deb and Garry at the Mackerel Beach Hilton

the needle but a friendship ring is paramount to a surfie chick. Now that Debbie has one, she is fully fledged. So she accepts Garry's drug taking for the time being and by doing so gains an advantage. She is now in a position to make a demand on him. They have been going around for four months but at this point she is still a virgin. It's an abnormal predicament for a Greenhills Gang girl to find herself in. Sure, Debbie knows that surfing comes first, girls second. That's the accepted code. As they say in the book, 'It was waves, then babes'.[49] But Debbie now wants to lose her virginity like all the other girls. At an abandoned fibro shack which they dub 'the Mackerel Beach Hilton', she confronts Garry with a line that will recur in a later scene: 'Surfing, that's all you ever think about'. If Garry's increasing dependence on drugs hasn't quashed his sex drive then now is the time to prove it. He puts aside the cocaine that he purchased with the proceeds from hocking his father's cassette player and draws Debbie towards him for a pash. This is the image used on the poster and I nearly fainted when I saw it blown up on an

Debbie feels 'it' inside her

enormous billboard above the Village Cinema in George Street, Sydney. Behind the scenes I was having a torrid romance with my on-screen love interest. We were method acting, I guess you could call it, so the intimacy was for real. Still, stripping off and getting it on in front of an entire film crew was confronting.

We find the couple in bed the next morning and Debbie asks Garry to give 'it' to her and she'll 'throw it away'. 'It', as we learn, is a condom. Again our teens are depicted practising safe sex. But when they look for 'it', it's not there. Suddenly Debbie feels something inside her. The condom has come off and the all too predictable consequences of this will occupy the next phase of the film.

The pair next meet in a playground and Debbie announces that her periods are overdue. Here we are in kiddie land discussing a very adult theme. It reminds us that these characters are still only kids themselves. As I mentioned earlier, I was three or four years older than Debbie was in the book and well past puberty, which for me, occurred when I was eleven. I may have been a bit too old for the role, as some critics observed, but I could certainly relate closely to what my character was going through.

So, what were the options for a girl in Debbie's predicament? Without any proper sex education at school or at home, she is incredibly ill-informed. 'When Cheryl's overdue she rides her horse bare-back', she says, spelling out what it says in the book: 'Cheryl was always galloping Randy, unsaddled, around the football field'.[50] Then Debbie suggests another dubious method of getting rid of an unwanted foetus: 'some of the girls get Strach to punch them in the stomach'.

To a film that's been described as both a comedy and 'a solid piece of gritty realism' this scene adds another dimension, that of educational aid.[51] A study guide was, in fact, issued to coincide with the film's release in which this particular scene is discussed as a way of getting students to talk about these issues:

> Neither of them are equipped to handle the problem of teenage pregnancy, and the point is made implicitly in the scene, that neither of them has had the advantage of responsibly-presented sex education, either at home or at school. They are both victims of a conservative morality that has preferred to ignore their adolescent sexuality, rather than come to grips with a facet of their lives that is undeniably real.[52]

The film makes it clear that Debbie has no one to turn to for expert advice. Forced to go shopping for a new car with her parents who are trying to cheer her up, Debbie can think only about finding the nearest toilet. She sits, peers down and, seeing no sign of menstrual blood, slouches back despondently. According to Kelly, this very female scenario was something in the script that initially appalled Beresford:

> Bruce just thought that was so disgusting. He kept going, 'Oh, nobody wants to know anything about that' and I said, 'Maybe you don't but trust me, every female in the audience will relate to a girl running to the toilet to see whether her period has come if she thinks she's pregnant'.

It happens again in the next scene when the family celebrates the acquisition of their new car in the local Pizza Hut restaurant. Debbie heads for the toilet to see if there has been any change. Later, unable to sleep she goes once more. Beresford might have been reluctant to include these scenes in the film but girls and women in the audience can certainly relate. Meaghan Morris described them as 'the best scenes I have ever seen in any film about the basic mechanics of pregnancy scares'.[53]

When Debbie finally goes to Garry's house for help, his mother tells her that he is up in his room studying but she finds him splayed out on his bed in a drugged up state. Again, the parents are totally oblivious to the condition of their offspring. All alone with her adult dilemma Debbie stops in front of a surf shop to admire the boards. We see her through the glass from inside, as we often do when the director wants to accentuate her feeling of alienation. If only she was a boy she wouldn't have to deal with this, the most depressing side effect of puberty. And what's more, if she was a boy she could surf.

Debbie has the puberty blues big time and takes a day off school. Rising from her sick bed she pays one more visit to the toilet, but this time, instead of becoming even bluer by the sight of her knickers, she is overjoyed. We don't see it but we know it's menstrual blood, proof finally that she is not pregnant. She slumps back with relief. This is one of my favourite moments in the film.

Debbie is now a different person altogether. Her brush with pregnancy has strengthened her sense of self and, with her newfound confidence, she is about to challenge the entire Gang. It's raining and everyone is gathered inside. The boys are focused on a game of cards when Vicki and Cheryl emerge from the kitchen proudly carrying a lop-sided cake with toxic green icing dribbled all over it. They wait for a response to their handiwork work but it is not forthcoming. Resigned to their subservient roles the girls place the cake down in front of the boys and watch contentedly as they hoe into it with their hands. Without even taking their eyes off the game, they wipe their mouths and Strach hands the plate back.

In response to this scene Morris wrote that 'the impression of a cinematic cliché is a bit too strong to be persuasive'.[54] But it does make the point that Debbie is disgusted by the boy's display of animal behaviour. She tries to motivate some action by suggesting a drive. 'Yeah', says Seagull, 'we could go check out the waves'. This really pisses Debbie off. 'All you're interested in is surfing', she says, echoing the statement she made to Garry at the Mackerel Beach Hilton, and for the first time in the entire scene the boys lift their eyes from the card game and turn to stare at her. The other Gang girls look incredulous too. She was accepted into this clique after much crawling and grovelling on the understanding that girls' desires don't enter into the equation and now she wants to change the rules? Again we see her through the glass of a rainy window. She's revealed herself as an outsider with very different aspirations to the Gang. But it will take one more nudge to tip her over the edge and it happens one night at the mall. Debbie and the other Gang girls suddenly become aware of a commotion nearby. Suspecting it must be someone famous they go to inspect but when they arrive at the scene they find ambulance attendants lifting a lifeless looking Garry onto a trolley. It's been a rapid decline for the once healthy surfie and it's the absolute last straw for our Deb.

In one of the most dramatic images in the whole film we now see black smoke billowing from a bonfire on Cronulla Beach. It's an improvised surfie funeral using details from the book about a similar service, coupled with a ritual sacrifice to the God of the Seas, King Huey, to get the surf pumping.[55] For Sandra Hall the whole thing was a bit forced:

> Much is made of the death of Debbie's boy friend... there's even a memorial bonfire on the beach for him. Yet Garry has been seen to be dying for some time by everybody including Debbie and his mother, and nobody has done a thing about

One of the most dramatic images of the film: the beach funeral

> the approaching tragedy. So while the bonfire looks handsome, and is a useful gimmick for bringing about the denouement, it is never more than just a gimmick added to the tale of *Puberty Blues*.[56]

Nevertheless, it is the only time we see any emotion from the otherwise undemonstrative boys. As they paddle out to offer up Garry's board to the ocean Debbie watches from the shore. 'It stinks', she says to Sue who has come up beside her. It's a major revelation for her character and the camera zooms in on her face to accentuate it. A tear rolls from her eye and, as if by some divine intervention, the sun breaks through, illuminating her face. The shot freezes then slowly fades to black.

It's a brand new sunny day, and indeed a whole new wonderful world for our bosom buddies when the next shot fades up. A gaggle of grommets are hanging outside the surfboard shop where Debbie previously dallied to admire the boards. Now we see her and Sue emerge from the shop carrying one of their own, spray-painted with a pouncing tiger. These chicks mean business. The sight of them elicits a barrage of derisive cries from the grommets but the young women remain defiant. The abuse continues as they walk up Cronulla beach; and in the film's very last visit to the dunny, one person even cries out 'Ya toilets!'. For Mudie Cunningham this line sums up the whole white trash aesthetic of the film. As it happens, it's a line that was contributed by a friend who came in to help with some post-synching. She was a prefect at the private girls school that I went to, and not at all your typical white trash, yet this was something she felt compelled to yell out in the spur of the moment. What is it about this film and toilets?

Recalling the very first scene in which Debbie called Freda a 'moll', both girls now stop in their tracks to say 'hi' to her. They are finally redeeming themselves by rejecting the sexist Greenhills code and supporting the sisterhood instead. Freda is shell-shocked but manages an excited acknowledgement in their wake. Audiences often laugh derisively at this contrivance but it does reveal a marked change in the girls. Debbie and Sue continue up the beach to Greenhills but this time they are different people—Debbie no longer wears blue but an optimistic shade of yellow. At the sight of their arrival, the Gang lets loose with the expected stream of abuse. 'Slack-arsed molls', 'Ya Westies,' Bruce even pipes up with the old chestnut 'Chicks don't surf!'.

The stirring finale music starts up with Sharon O'Neille singing

Tim Finn's hit song *Nobody Takes Me Seriously*, a rally to self-expression and independence. In slow motion Debbie paddles to catch a wave but doesn't make it on. She manages to get to her feet on the next wave but falls off and the Gang dismiss her as 'hopeless'. Now Debbie catches her first wave, riding it backhand in slow motion, which contrasts with the real time reactions of the Gang. Their condescending expressions gradually fall from their faces as Debbie proceeds to catch wave after wave, her boobs bouncing around in her tiny yellow bikini. Danny is the only one who appreciates her performance, rising to his feet to holler out 'Good one!' (I remember Tony Hughes insisting on this response to a sceptical Beresford). The rest of the Gang are simply gob-smacked as are most of the film's audiences.

That Debbie actually triumphs in this male dominated sports arena in full view of her peer group instantly renders the entire Greenhills Gang impotent. Everything they have stood for is rejected in this moment. It is a supremely feminist statement and, as academic Lesley Speed writes: 'Even today, many female spectators experience a sense of exhilaration when the jeers of onlookers in the film are subdued by Debbie's display of her surfing ability.'[57] Albie Thoms notes this 'feminist line' in his book *Surfmovies*:

> This symbol of surfing as a form of personal liberation had been used for men many times before, but its re-use here for women was timely, since feminist issues ... were dominating Australian social discourse, and it proved to have particular relevance to the surfing subculture where male chauvinism continued to dominate.[58]

For my part, I revelled in the chance to show off a few moves and escape the crew for a while. I used my own board emblazoned with a pink jelly fish and, under Beresford's direction, smiled as much as possible—tricky given that I had three stiches in my foot. I had jumped over a barbed wire regeneration fence on my way to take a pee in the sand dunes and had gashed it open. Thankfully this little hitch doesn't deter from the spirit of the moment which still makes me smile whenever I see it.

Liberated from the Gang and its backward conventions, Debbie and Sue are revealed in the golden light of sunset as the camera cranes up over the sand dune to find them high above the beach and indeed the whole suburb of Cronulla. They survey the scene from this elevated position. They're above it all now. It's been a great day and Sue suspects that they've been dropped. 'Who cares?' replies Debbie and Sue agrees, 'Yeah, who cares'. The shot freezes right there on the two of them laughing off their puberty blues. The theme song starts up and the credits roll.

6

PUBES

In just 87 minutes, this episodic story has seen our girls struggle to get accepted by their peer group, gain entrance to the Gang, get wised up about its overall insignificance in the grand scheme of things and finally defy it. That's the story arc. Debbie and Sue are together at the end as they are at the beginning, having experienced their surfie saga together. They have turned their backs on the Gang and have literally survived because, as we read in the stark epilogue to the book, many of its members didn't. Two died from drug-related incidents, eight developed heroin habits, several landed in jail and others had breakdowns. And the fate of some, like Freda, were simply listed as 'unknown'.

Germaine Greer acknowledges the girls' narrow escape in her foreword:

> Debbie and Sue are the only ones among their peers to reject their slavish dependence on the boys and motivate themselves to accomplish something before the options are inexorably cancelled one by one. Gabrielle Carey and Kathy Lette don't tell us how they did it; if we want to motivate our children to follow their example, we cannot leave it to dumb luck.

But Lette did suggest a reason why she and Carey managed to avoid the fate that befell the rest of the Gang when she said simply: 'If we hadn't had each other we may never have got out'.[59] It was that bond, that deep, supportive friendship that gave them the strength they needed to get the hell out of there. And this is the big lesson for teenage audiences, especially girls—that they can do this too, they don't have to take the sort of shit that kids like those in the Greenhills Gang dish up. It's a strong feminist message and one that has relevance today.

The film had a special premiere at the Cronulla Cinema on the 29th of November 1981 and Lette was in attendance. A reporter interviewed her in the foyer where she was nervously looking for her parents. 'They refused to read the book', she said, 'because it caused such a sensation in their local area when it came out. They agreed to come along today but I was watching them all through it and they were just tense, rigid'.[60] Kathy's mother, remember, was headmistress at a local school and appalled by her daughter's revelations. But she would have to acknowledge the impact of the film as it began to break box office records around the country. As would countless other mothers. 'When we were filming anywhere in the area, we had mothers coming up and saying "How could you?"' revealed Kelly.

> You could pick them, grabbing any member of the crew who would then point at either Joan or I and they'd come storming up and say 'How could you be involved with this filth?' We'd say, 'If you wait and see the film, you'll see that it's actually an anti-drug story.' We just got harassed everywhere, absolutely everywhere.

While the book generated a lot of antagonism, especially from parents who didn't want to accept the reality it documented or their possible contribution to it, it also fostered a fan club of teenagers who flocked to see the film version. Just before it officially opened at a 10 am session at the Village Cinema in Melbourne on 10 December 1981, the producers received a call from Alan Finney of Roadshow Distributors saying that they had already sold out the first session and kids were lining up for tickets for the second, which was also about to sell out. 'It was unbelievable' Kelly recalls.

> I still remember the sense of excitement of 'Oh my god, everybody said it was going to be a hit and it is'. It was amazing. A lot of people had said, but kids only pay half price and Alan Finney said, 'Yeah, but they're repeat audience. It doesn't matter if they only pay half price, they keep coming back and they keep paying.'

And they did, some boasting that they'd seen it up to ten times.

Not being an investor in the film I was much more interested in the reviews. Mostly they were favourable. John Lapsley of the Sydney *Sun Herald* called it 'a wonderfully judged film about the comedy and tragedy of growing up'. John Hinde of the *National Times* wrote: 'All up *Puberty Blues* turns out to be a brave and important film'. In Adelaide, Terry Jennings of the *Advertiser* said: 'After years of being starved of identifiable, recognisable images of themselves, here is a feast for adolescents'. While Wayne Webster of Sydney's *Daily Telegraph* commented: 'The movie doesn't pull any punches as it exposes the funny and tragic sides of growing up... At times it is almost like watching yourself'. It certainly was for me. And for my efforts *Playboy* magazine voted me Best New Actress.

Kelly and Long flew to America to secure a distribution deal for the film and found a young lawyer called Joe Peckerman who

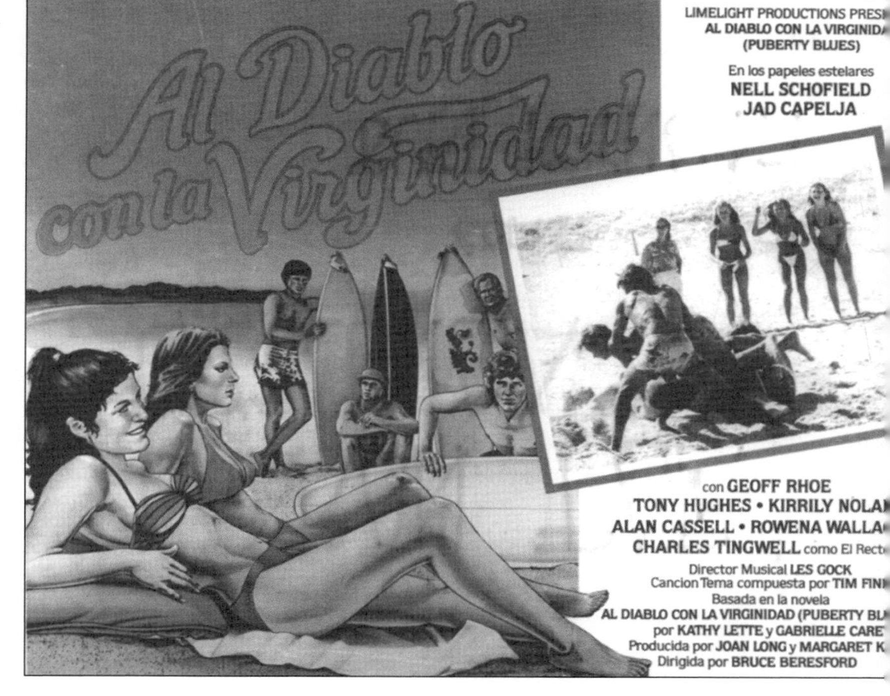

The Spanish poster for *Puberty Blues*

loved it. With his help they made their first sale to 20th Century Fox, which in one fell swoop, covered the entire budget. They paid back all their investors, big and small, and went straight into a healthy profit. 20th Century Fox then sold the film all over the world and strange posters began appearing from places like Germany where they depicted Debbie as a sort of Lolita character in big red heart shaped glasses licking a green ice cream, and from Spain where they retitled it *Al Diablo con la Virginidad.* For

Kelly's part, she went out and paid cash for a sports car—a silver Datsun 180—with her first profit cheque.

And still the money kept rolling in. For one of the lowest budget films around it was doing pretty well. The box office gross was $3,918,000 in the first year and that was before U.S. and Australian TV sales. The film was being hailed as the biggest Australian film of all time along with *Mad Max 2* and *Gallipoli,* both of which opened at around the same time. On the publicity tour that accompanied its release, Jad and I found ourselves on the same circuit as Mel Gibson and Mark Lee who were promoting *Gallipoli* and we all spent a fun night together in the hotel drinking the mini bars dry. In late January 1982 Jad and I were invited along with Joan Long to attend the Manila Film Festival, an initiative of the then first lady, Imelda Marcos. Although not an official entry, *Puberty Blues* attracted a lot of attention. Newspaper reports claimed that 4,000 people queued for two hours to get into the cinema and there was a scary moment after the screening when Jad and I were mobbed by a large percentage of them all seeking autographs. Suddenly we were celebrities, flying around in Lear Jets and cutting the rug with Imelda and her special guests including actor George Hamilton and the new hot sexpot screen siren Pia Zadora.

The film was launched onto the American market alongside *The Road Warrior (Mad Max 2)* in July 1983 at the Lincoln Plaza Theatre. By this time Beresford had made *Tender Mercies,* his first American film, and audiences were keen to see his back catalogue. In *The New York Times,* David Elliot commented:

> there have been many movies about teenagers, and some about surfers... (the most notable and pompous was *Big Wednesday* in 1978). *Puberty Blues* is the first to bind those elements inside

On set of the movie that reflects the consequences of the co-education system

> a female point of view, and make us feel the special agony of what that can mean... Visually beautiful, piercingly accurate, it's one of the best movies yet made about teenagers.[61]

Dilys Powell in Britain's *Punch* magazine was less enthusiastic in her review of the film which opened in London on August 19 1982:

> It isn't so much a sex-game as an Australian *Gregory's Girl,* [a sweet and very funny Scottish flick about a gawky teen boy's growing sexual awareness] but to an English audience a great deal less amusing. One emerges, though, with one basic conviction. If the movie reflects the consequences of the co-education system which is seeping into the old-world practices

> of this country, one can be grateful to have known the days when school was for solemn games and the passing of examinations.[62]

Powell's comments aside, this depiction of contemporary life in the colony of New South Wales made a big splash around the world. After the initial rush settled down, the film found itself a place in school curricula as a discussion starter in Personal Development classes and the producers won an Australian Teachers Of Media Award for their services to the cause. The film continues to be used as a tool in High Schools and other institutions. Courses in Media Studies use it to prompt analysis of such things as 'The Australian Way of Life in the 1970s' providing, as it does, a snapshot of that era. It has become an important social document encapsulating a certain Aussie way of life that is a constant source of amusement—and education—to audiences. Nearly twenty years later film writer Joshua Smith wrote that:

> *Puberty Blues,* like many films seen to belong to the teen film sub-genre, was largely ignored by the critical community at the time of its release, and thought of as a comedy. In hindsight, the film can be read as both a dark, brooding, analysis of Australia's attempts to break away from its colonial heritage and as one of Australia's most confronting and honest feminist works.[63]

The film has had many screenings on Australian television over the years, firstly on Channel 7 then on Pay TV's Comedy Channel, which ran a promo calling it 'the Australian cult classic'. It remains a touchstone and is referred to regularly to illustrate the trials of being a teenager. ABC television's popular culture show, *Mondo Thingo,* used it to comment on Catherine

Hardwicke's hard-hitting teen movie, *Thirteen,* also based on a real-life story:

> Trying to fit in is the unending agony of every generation of teenagers and for the '80s generation of Australian girls this was captured by the book and then film *Puberty Blues*... [the film] is very much of its time and is deeply bedded in surfie culture but remains relevant to teens today. It's also a time capsule snapshot of some great Aussie slang.

Also referencing the real-life gang rape and murder story in Steven Vidler's *Blackrock,* and Ivan Sen's moving portrayal of two Aboriginal teenagers in *Beneath Clouds,* the reporter noted:

> Each of these films takes a different path but the obstacles faced in them are essentially the same. They might make you hold your own children a bit closer or make you decide not to have children at all.[64]

Despite having experienced the trials depicted in the film first hand, Lette and Carey both decided to have children of their own. Twenty years after sitting down to write their surfie saga, Carey saw an amateur stage production of the work. It was, she wrote, 'a much darker version than the screen adaptation' and she found it

> shocking. The story is one of cruelty, self-destruction and rape. What I found most distressing was all those nice, middle-class girls—sensitive, educated and intelligent—[were] still at the mercy of those brutish boys. Afterwards I spoke to some of the actors, who told me how much they could identify with the book. 'Tell me it's not that bad now' I pleaded in vain. The sad thing for me is just how relevant *Puberty Blues* still is. Kathy Lette and I certainly didn't write it with that in mind. We wrote it with the intention, somewhat naïve, somewhat noble, that we could change things.[65]

Obviously there have been some changes in Australian youth culture over the past quarter of a century. As Carey points out,

> If there's one thing you can say with any certainty about the younger generation, it's that they're more conservative than we were. And although I find that a little sad—the lack of activism among university students, for example, suggests to me a lack of idealism—perhaps, in terms of drugs, it is a real positive.

In her foreword to the book, however, Germaine Greer notes that drug use is even more prevalent among the younger generation today:

> Hanging out is more likely to involve alcohol, ecstasy, smoking and casual sex in the twenty-first century than it was in the 1970s. The only lifestyle worth living is hedonistic, and the only pleasurable exploits open to young teenagers involve breaking the law, one way or another.[66]

So what's new? How much have things really shifted?

One thing's for sure, there has definitely been a huge change in the ocean—an incredible sea change, in fact. Chicks are out there surfing in numbers like never before. There are now over 200,000 female surfers carving up the waves around the country's coastline according to *Surfing Australia*. Last year alone 160,000 girls participated in surf schools and that number can only get bigger. As I sat at my desk, method-writing in my scraggy fluoro 'Bad Girl Surf Angel' singlet, revisiting my role in the film, it dawned on me that instead of trying to live it down, maybe I needed to live up to it.

I decided to go back to where it all began, back to my soul surfing teenage stomping ground. I packed up the car and headed off on a surfing safari, admittedly without a board, but I wanted to get back into that head space, barefoot on a pristine Pacific beach with dolphins plunging around in the crystal waves. After setting up camp in the rainforest behind the sand dunes my friend and I got stuck into creating a full-on surfie scrag look by cutting up vintage Bell's Beach Pro Am T-shirts and the like. As the Manly-based surfer Louise Southerden writes in *Surf's Up: The Girl's Guide to Surfing*, 'Looking good when surfing is important to many women'.[67] From out of the bush came an all-singing soul-surfin' Jesus freak named Garth. As fate would have it, he had just fixed up his spare board in the hope that he would bump into a surfie chick keen for a wave. Well, I was out there with my new surfing guru in a flash, decked out in my shocking pink board shorts and fluoro green zinc. It all came flooding back: the feeling of liberation, of being at one with nature, with no one else on the beach except us. Large fish were surfing with me under the shapely white board and I was feeling young again. Garth even told me I was 'redeemable'. It was almost as good as being 'rootable'.

Garth left me with strict instructions to surf at least once a week: 'It's good for your soul', he explained. So back in the Big Smoke I bought myself an old surfboard at the Bondi markets, a classic Town and Country made in Lennox Head and decorated with no less than four yin and yang symbols. Then a friend told me about a surf camp she'd been on at, wait for it, Cronulla Beach. She'd seen an ad for the women-only camp in the publication *Lesbians on the Loose* so I grabbed a copy and called them up. I 'fessed up that I was researching a book on this old movie that I had been in, shot right there where they were teaching 'packers the ropes. 'Oh my God!' screamed Meagan, the co-owner of the company, 'You're our main selling point! You can come for free!'

In all those years that the film had been doing the rounds I never did see any money but now here I was getting a fabulous freebie. And what's more, we would be surfing at Greenhills! As their information sheet reported

> Greenhills is... the surfing site of the late 1970s book and early 1980s classic Australian Surf film *Puberty Blues* (you know, 'Girls don't surf', apparently! Quite ironic really considering these days we are an all girls instructing team and Australia's only lesbian owned and operated surf school and surf tour company operating under permit at Greenhills, ha, who would've thought...)

This was the first time I'd been back to Cronulla since shooting the film and the very first time I'd been to Greenhills. The crew had never ventured that far up the beach because it was logistically impossible to transport all the gear there. So I was like an excited kid when I rocked up to the meeting point at Kurnell. I was the first to arrive and admittedly I was a bit embarrassed when the others came and it slowly dawned on them who I was: every single one of the eight women had seen the film. and each of them wanted me to pose for a photo. Why not? Greenhills was a revelation: the beautiful water, the remote sand dunes and the massive waves pumping out on the reefs. After some instruction we hit the water on big Malibu foam boards. I was straight out the back taking off on everything I could paddle onto. You can take the chick out of the surf but you can't take the surf out of the chick.

Puberty Blues started a trend. It was one of the first films to feature females surfing since the phenomenon of the *Gidget* series in the late 1950s and early 1960s but unlike those films it had a strong feminist line. It would be nearly twenty years before another

Shaking off the puberty blues

surf film anything like it came along. As Andrew Humphreys wrote in the *Sydney Morning Herald,* 'outside of the final five minutes of *Puberty Blues* the only other movie to feature female surfers is *Blue Crush*'.[68] This told the story of a Hawaiian surfie chick and her bosom buddies preparing for the women's Pipe Masters surfing competition. The protagonist had to overcome her fear of the ultra gnarly Pipeline waves and audiences were treated to some awesome surfing as she did so. Parts of it were constructed using computer generated imagery with the heroine's face inserted onto another girl's body, a much more modern method than the old *Gidget* days when surfing was often filmed using rear projection.

It feels good to have done all my own surfing in *Pubes* and if it inspired women to get in to the ocean and feel the freedom and excitement of riding a wave, I'm even more chuffed. Chicks *can* bloody well surf, as six times world champion Layne Beachley has proven beyond a shadow of a doubt. In March 2004, in what was described as a 'battle of the sexes' the Sydney born champ pitted herself against the men's world champion Andy Irons amongst other blokes at the Energy Australia Open at Newcastle Beach. What's more, she's hunting the illusive 100 foot wave and Billabong's cash prize of $1,000 per foot for riding it. Go girlfriend!

NOTES

1 *Get The Picture*, Sydney: Australian Film Commission, 2003
2 Author's interview with Kathy Lette, 16 July 2004. All quotes from Lette from this source unless otherwise stated.
3 'The Big Chill', *Australian Story*, ABC TV, 30 September 2002
4 Kathy Lette and Gabrielle Carey, *Puberty Blues*, London: Picador, 2002, p. 3
5 Stephen Cooney, 'Nell Charlotte Schofield and Emma Charlotte Bromfield' *(sic)* in *Sea Notes*, April/May 1978.
6 www.morningoftheeart.net
7 Author's interview with Margaret Kelly, 29 February 2004. All quotes from Kelly from this source unless otherwise stated.
8 Susan Dermody and Elizabeth Jacka, *The Screening of Australia Vol 2: Anatomy of a National Cinema* Sydney: Currency Press, 1988
9 Tom O'Regan, *Australian National Cinema*, London: Routledge, 1996
10 *Four Corners*, ABC TV 1979 (used in *Australian Story* 2002)
11 Geraldine Pascall, 'Tax Relief Set to Break the Local Film Drought', *Sydney Morning Herald*, c. January 1981. Sourced from author's mouldy scrap book so exact date unknown.
12 Ibid
13 Miranda Brown, 'Pubert Blues, Margaret Kelly and Joan Long' in *Cinema Papers*, Nov/Dec 1981
14 David Stratton, *The Avocado Plantation – Boom and Bust in the Australian Film Industry*. Sydney: Pan Macmillan, 1990
15 Interview with Bruce Beresford, *Puberty Blues DVD*, Umbrella Productions.
16 Evan Williams, 'For Esme – with lots of squalor', from author's scrapbook; exact source unknown.
17 Lette and Carey, *Puberty Blues*, p. 112
18 From author's scrapbook. Exact source unknown.
19 Author's interview with Don McAlpine, 27 June 2004
20 J. Daniels, *Absolute Goldmine of Aussie Trash One Liners*, www.us.imdb.com, 25 April 2001
21 Lette and Carey, *Puberty Blues*, p. 28
22 Ibid, p. 5
23 Frank Hurley, veteran cinematographer of two of the most remarkable Antarctic expeditions, headed up a four camera unit to shoot the recreation of the legendary cavalry charge of Australia's Light Horse Brigade at Beersheba in the First World War in *Forty Thousand Horsemen*.

24 Lette and Carey, *Puberty Blues*, p 29
25 Ibid, p 21
26 You hear the term 'box-tosser' in Beresford's earlier film, *Barry McKenzie Holds His Own*, when Bazza uses it to describe an air hostess on the charmingly named 'Frog Air'.
27 Brown, *Cinema Papers*
28 Tobacco In Australia: Facts and Issues, www.quit.org.au/quit/Fandl/welcome.htm
29 Author's interview with Daniel Mudie Cunningham, 11 February 2004
30 Lette and Carey, *Puberty Blues*, p 8
31 Mudie-Cunningham believes the film suggests this.
32 Sandra Hall, 'The surfie girls of Cronulla', *The Bulletin*, 5 January 1982
33 Elizabeth Riddell, 'Puberty Blues – a lot going for it', *Theatre Australia*, February 1982
34 *The Big Chill*, 'Australian Story'
35 Lette and Carey, *Puberty Blues*, London: Picador, 2002
36 Kylie Minogue 'Foreword' in *Puberty Blues*, p ix
37 Germaine Greer 'Foreword' in Lette and Carey *Puberty Blues*, p xi
38 Lette and Carey, *Puberty Blues*, pp 2-3
39 Ibid, p 51
40 Ibid, p 38
41 Gabrielle Carey, 'I'm Not as Bad as You were Mum', *Sydney Morning Herald*, 12 October 2000
42 Carey and Lette, *Puberty Blues*, p 67
43 Ibid, p 73
44 'The Big Chill', *Australian Story*,
45 Derek Hynd, 'The Mongrel – Tracing the bastard bloodlines of the Australian surf animal', Episode 1, *Tracks*, April 2004
46 Germaine Greer, 'Grubby sex has just become a bit noisier' in *Sydney Morning Herald*, March 23 2004
47 Meaghan Morris, 'Sex through ploy in Puberty Blues and the French Lieutenant's Woman', in the *Financial Review*, 11 December 1981
48 Jim Schembri, 'Puberty Blues' in *Cinema Papers*, January/February 1982
49 Lette and Carey, *Puberty Blues*, p 28
50 Ibid, p 105
51 See Ann Gul's review in Scott Murray, ed, *Australian Film 1978-1994*, Melbourne: Oxford University Press, 1995, p 81
52 Barbara Boyd-Anderson, *Puberty Blues: a study guide*, Carlton South: Australian Teachers of Media in conjunction with the Australian Film Commission and Roadshow Distributors, 1981
53 Morris, 'Sex Through Ploy in

Puberty Blues and the French Lieutenant's Woman'
54 Ibid
55 Lette and Carey, *Puberty Blues*, p 55
56 Hall, 'The surfie girls of Cronulla'
57 Speed, 'You and me against the world: revisiting Puberty Blues', *Metro*, No. 140
58 Albie Thoms, *Surfmovies: the history of the surf film in Australia*, Noosa Heads: Shore Thing Publishing, 2000
59 'The Big Chill', *Australian Story*,
60 Geraldine Brooks 'The Puberty Blues Mob: Mercs, Volvos 'n UBDs' in *The Good Weekend*, 5 December 1981
61 David Elliot, '*Puberty Blues*: one of best ever at capturing teens' special agony' in the *New York Times*, 10 July 1983
62 Dilys Powell, 'Bruce's Sheilas' in *Punch*, 25 August 1982
63 Joshua Smith, '*Puberty Blues* – all too real' on *Oz Cinema – Your Guide To Australian Film*, 12 May 1998, published on website www.ozcinema.com
64 *Mondo Thingo*, ABC TV, March 2004
65 Gabrielle Carey, 'I'm Not As Bad As You Were Mum'
66 Germaine Greer, 'Foreword' in Lette and Carey, *Puberty Blues*
67 Louise Southerden, *Surf's Up: The Girl's Guide to Surfing*, Sydney: Allen and Unwin, 2003
68 Andrew Humphreys, 'View From the Couch' in *Good Weekend* 6 December 2003

BIBLIOGRAPHY

Get The Picture, Sydney: Australian Film Commission, 2003

Brown, Miranda, 'Puberty Blues, Margaret Kelly and Joan Long' in *Cinema Papers*, Nov/Dec 1981

Boyd-Anderson, Barbara, *Puberty Blues: a study guide*, Carlton South: Australian Teachers of Media in conjunction with the Australian Film Commission and Roadshow Distributors, 1981

Brooks, Geraldine, 'The Puberty Blues Mob: Mercs, Volvos 'n UBDs' *The Good Weekend*, 5 December 1981

Carey, Gabrielle, 'I'm Not as Bad as You were Mum', *Sydney Morning Herald*, 12 October 2002

Cooney, Stephen, 'Nell Charlotte Schofield and Emma Charlotte Bromfield (sic)' in *Sea Notes*, April/May 1978

Daniels, J. 'Absolute Goldmine of Aussie Trash One Liners', www.us.imdb.com, 25 April 2001

Dermody, Susan and Elizabeth Jacka, *The Screening of Australia Vol 2: Anatomy of a National Cinema* Sydney: Currency Press, 1988

Elliot, David, '*Puberty Blues*: one of best ever at capturing teens' special agony' in the *New York Times*, 10 July 1983

Gaskin, Ina May, *Spiritual Midwifery*, Summertown, TN: Book Pub. Co, 1976

Greer, Germaine, 'Grubby sex has just become a bit noisier' in *Sydney Morning Herald*, 23 March 2004

Gul, Ann, in Scott Murray, ed, *Australian Film 1978-1994*, Melbourne: Oxford University Press, 1995

Hall, Sandra, 'The surfie girls of Cronulla', *The Bulletin*, 5 January 1982

Humphreys, Andrew, 'View From the Couch', *Good Weekend* 6 December 2003

Hynd, Derek, 'The Mongrel – Tracing the bastard bloodlines of the Australian surf animal', Episode 1, *Tracks*, April 2004

Lette, Kathy and Gabrielle Carey, *Puberty Blues*, London: Picador, 2002

McMahon, Elizabeth, 'From Puberty Blues to Blue Crush: Feminist fiction at the Beach', Paper delivered in April, 2004 at Sydney University

Morris, Meaghan, 'Sex through ploy in Puberty Blues and the French Lieutenant's Woman', in *Financial Review*, 11 December 1981

O'Regan, Tom, *Australian National Cinema*, London: Routledge, 1996

Pascall, Geraldine, 'Tax Relief Set to Break the Local Film Drought', *Sydney Morning Herald*, c. January 1981.

Powell, Dilys, 'Bruce's Sheilas', *Punch*, 25 August 1982

Riddell, Elizabeth, 'Puberty Blues – a lot going for it', *Theatre Australia*, February 1982

Schembri, Jim, 'Puberty Blues' in *Cinema Papers*, January/February 1982

Smith, Joshua, '*Puberty Blues* – all too real' on *Oz Cinema – Your Guide To Australian Film*, 12 May 1998, www.ozcinema.com

Southerden, Louise, *Surf's Up: The Girl's Guide to Surfing*, Sydney: Allen and Unwin, 2003

Speed, Lesley, 'You and Me Against the World: Revisiting Puberty Blues', *Metro*, No. 140

Stratton, David, *The Avocado Plantation – Boom and Bust in the Australian Film Industry*. Sydney: Pan Macmillan, 1990

Thoms, Albie, *Surfmovies: the history of the surf film in Australia*, Noosa Heads: Shore Thing Publishing, 2000

White, Patrick, *The Tree of Man*, Ringwood, Vic.: Penguin Books, 1961

Williams, Evan, 'For Esme – with lots of squalor', author's scrapbook

FILMOGRAPHY

The Adventures of Barry McKenzie, Bruce Beresford, 1972
Barry McKenzie Holds His Own, Bruce Beresford, 1974
Beneath Clouds, Ivan Sen, 2002
Big Wednesday, John Milius, 1978
Blackrock, Steven Vidler, 1997
Blue Crush, John Stockwell, 2002
Breaker Morant, Bruce Beresford, 1980
Caddie, Donald Crombie, 1976
The Cars That Ate Paris, Peter Weir, 1974
The Club, Bruce Beresford, 1980
Crystal Voyager, David Elfick, 1971
David and Pywaket, Donald Wynne, c. 1970
Division 4 (TV Series), Colin Eggleston and George Miller, 1969
Don's Party, Bruce Beresford, 1976
Easy Rider, Dennis Hopper, 1969
Fast Times at Ridgemont High, Amy Heckerling, 1981
Forty Thousand Horsemen, Charles Chauvel, 1940
Gallipoli, Peter Weir, 1981
The Getting of Wisdom, Bruce Beresford, 1977
Gidget, Paul Wendkos, 1959
Greetings From Wollongong, Mary Callaghan, 1981
Gregory's Girl, Bill Forsyth, 1981
Homicide (TV Series), Graeme Arthur et al, 1964
Hot Lips and Inner Tubes, Yuri Farrant, 1975

The triumphant surfie chicks

Mad Max 2 (The Road Warrior), George Miller, 1981
Mondo Thingo, George Dodd, 2004
Morning of the Earth, Albert Falzon, 1972
My Brilliant Career, Gillian Armstrong, 1979
Palm Beach, Albie Thoms, 1980
The Passionate Industry, Joan Long, 1973
Picnic at Hanging Rock, Peter Weir, 1975
The Picture Show Man, John Power, 1977

The Pictures That Moved: Australian Cinema 1896 – 1920, Joan Long, 1969
Pig in a Poke (TV Series), Michael Jenkins, 1977
The Road Warrior (see *Mad Max 2*)
The Rocky Horror Picture Show, Jim Sharman, 1975
Star Struck, Gillian Armstrong, 1981
Summer City, Christopher Fraser, 1977
Tender Mercies, Bruce Beresford, 1983
Thirst, Rod Hardy, 1979
Thirteen, Catherine Hardwicke, 2004
Tubular Swells, Dick Hoole and Jack McCoy, 1976

On the set of *Puberty Blues*

CREDITS

Production Year
1981

Key Crew

Director
Bruce Beresford

Director of Photography
Don McAlpine (A.C.S.)

Screenplay
Margaret Kelly
Based on the novel *Puberty Blues* by Kathy Lette and Gabrielle Carey

Producers
Joan Long, Margaret Kelly

Film editors
William Anderson, Jeanine Chialvo

Sound Recordist
Gary Wilkins

Production Designer
David Copping

Wardrobe Mistress
Sue Armstrong

Musical director
Les Gock

Composers
Les Gock, Tim Finn

Production Manager
Greg Ricketson

First A.D.
Mark Egerton

Production Accountant
Penny Carl

Focus Puller
David Burr

Clapper Loader
Derry Field

Sound Assistant
Sue Kerr

Make-up
Judy Lovell

Continuity
Moya Iceton

Second A.D.
Marshall Crosby

Third A.D.
Renate Wilson

Gaffer
Rob Young

Best boy
Colin Williams

Production Secretary
Helen Watts

Location Managers
Phil Rich, Sue Parker

Casting
Alison Barrett

Stills
Mike Roll

Cast

Nell Schofield
Debbie

Jad Capelja
Sue

Geoff Rhoe
Garry

Tony Hughes
Danny

Sandy Paul
Tracey

Leander Brett
Cheryl

Jay Hackett
Bruce

Ned Lander
Strach

Joanne Olsen
Vicki

Julie Medana
Kim

Michael Shearman
Glenn

Dean Dunstone
Seagull

Tina Robinson
Freda

Nerida Clark
Carol

Kirrily Nolan
Mrs. Vickers

Alan Cassell
Mr. Vickers

Rowena Wallace
Mrs. Knight

Charles Tingwell
The Headmaster

Kate Shiel
Mrs. Yelland

Pamela Gibbons
Jazz Ballet Teacher

Lyn Murphy
Mrs. Hennessy

Andrew Martin
Mr. Berkhoff

Rob Thomas
Car Salesman

Brian Harrison
Mr. Little

Brian Anderson
Drive-in Attendant

ALSO AVAILABLE

The Mad Max Movies

'No other Australian films have influenced world cinema and popular culture as widely and lastingly as George Miller's *Mad Max* movies.' So writes ADRIAN MARTIN in this sparkling new appreciation of the movies that rudely shook up Australian cinema and made Mel Gibson and George Miller internationally famous. Martin compares the three *Mad Max* movies, sharing his views on which works best and why. In a chapter dedicated to each film, he looks at their critical reception and their themes, examines Miller's shooting techniques and provides a shot-by-shot analysis of integral scenes.

Since Mad Max roared onto cinema screens in 1979, the films have developed a worldwide cult following and provoked numerous debates as to their meaning: a study of masculinity in crisis, an investigation of good versus evil, a celebration of the Western (with wheels) or a frightening vision of the post-apocalypse. Martin explores these diverse interpretations in his fascinating account of three of Australia's most influential films.

Walkabout

Nicolas Roeg's *Walkabout* opened worldwide in 1971. Based on the novel of the same name, it is the story of two white children lost in the Australian Outback. They survive only through the help of an Aboriginal boy who is on walkabout during his initiation into manhood. The film earned itself a unique place in cinematic history and was re-released in 1998.

In this illuminating reflection on *Walkabout,* LOUIS NOWRA, one of Australia's leading dramatists and screenwriters, discusses Australia's iconic sense of the Outback and the peculiar resonance that the story of the lost child has in the Australian psyche. He tells how the film came to be made and how its preoccupations fit into the oeuvre of its director and cinematographer Nicolas Roeg and its screenwriter Edward Bond. Nowra identifies the film's distinctive take on a familiar story and its fable-like qualitities, while also exploring the film's relationship to Australia and its implications for the English society of its day. He recognises how relevant the film is to the contemporary struggle to try and find common ground between blacks and whites. *Walkabout*, says Nowra, 'destroyed the cliché of the Dead Heart and made us Australians see it from a unique perspective, as something wondrous, mysterious and sensuous. It took a stranger in a strange land to reveal it to us.'

Devil's Playground

Fred Schepisi's film, *The Devil's Playground*, is an intimate portrait of Tom, a thirteen-year-old struggling in spirit and body with the constraints of living in a Catholic seminary. It is also the story of the Brothers and how they cope with the demands of their faith. Made in 1976, this semi-autobiographical film established Schepisi as one of Australia's most talented directors and was one of the first Australian films to be selected for Directors' Fortnight at the Cannes Film Festival.

CHRISTOS TSIOLKAS invites you into his twenty-five year journey of viewing, re-viewing and re-imagining the film. He remembers his first illicit experience of the film at age thirteen and describes how his views of it changed in later years. As he chronicles the impact of *The Devil's Playground* on the development of his sense of self and of his love of cinema, he also explores the film in terms of sexuality, politics, history and aesthetics. Tsiolkas' account of what *The Devil's Playground* said, and didn't say, to him is a passionate tribute to the power of cinema.